I0521271

The Angel in Need
(The Freedom Church Series)

By Alex X. Bradbury

Copyright © 2018. All rights reserved. This book or any portion thereof may not be reproduced or used in any manner whatsoever without the express written permission of the author. All the characters of this work are fictional and any similarities to any real person or persons, living or dead, are coincidental and not intended by the author. While some places and/or entities are real, most are works of fiction and like persons, any similarities with places, businesses, or institutions are coincidental as well.

Quote

"The ultimate measure of a man is not where he stands in moments of comfort and convenience, but where he stands at times of challenge and controversy."

The Reverend Dr. Martin Luther King, Jr.

Before You Go Further

You might want to read the prequel series. Available as a prequel to the *Freedom Church Series* is the *Moore Family Series*, which are:

Book 1 - The Second Choice
Book 2 - A Matter of Trust
Book 3 - The Foodies
Book 4 - The Robin's Egg

All available now.

Plus with this book, you get the first chapter of the next book in the Freedom Church Series, "Josie's Journey".

Summary

Marcus and Millie Jenkins have a great life. Great ministry and jobs. House. Everything is almost perfect. But the one thing that they lack is children. Then one day, a stranger appears in their lives and turns everything upside down. Now, will they be able to keep this Angel when she's being hunted down by a criminal thug, who killed her mother. When one wayward stranger complicates things, as the second stranger will bring back dark secrets that both Marcus and Millie will have to face either separately or together. Will they survive it all? *The Angel in Need* is the first book in the Freedom Church Series by international selling author Alex X. Bradbury.

About Alex

Alex X. Bradbury is a pen name for an author of different genres. He has been an author, an educator in K-12 schools and colleges. He and his family reside in Ohio where 'Alex' enjoys swimming, writing, reading, and consulting. After a long career in education, Alex has recently decided to study to be a bi-vocational church leader and Bible educator.

Chapter 1
Millie
January

"What a dump!" Sofia says as we enter the old mansion for the first time since Freedom Church closed on the property transfer last month. The church, through a donation made by Jared and Amy Moore and others, acquired this abandoned mansion that sits across the street from Freedom Church. This mansion will become the *Sarah Moore House*, a women's shelter that I will run and operate with help from my friends. The mansion, located on the same street as the church is an old style brick, two-story house that was probably built in the late 1800s at the height of the population boom in the city. The house is in rough shape inside and Sofia is not exaggerating in saying it's a dump. Trash is strewn throughout the old abandoned house, with spray-painted colorful words decorating most of the rooms. The entrance way is large, and the first floor has a living room, two dens, a large dining room, and the kitchen in the old section of the first floor, with an addition made on the back for two additional bathroom suites that are accessible from the laundry area, off the kitchen. The second floor has one bathroom with six large bedrooms. The term 'mansion' may be an exaggeration. It's more like a large old house. The front is ornate with a wraparound porch facing the street. The driveway leads to the back where a detached carriage house is half-standing and has a hole in the roof. It's a home improvement show's dream fixer upper. Once finished, the house will base a counseling room and enough beds for five small families or four larger ones. It depends. The space needs flexibility and conveniences like multiple bathrooms. We're still in the planning stages though and various codes will need to be dealt with as well as serious demo work. Again, it's a fixer upper.   This converted house will be a testament to the legacy of my best friend, Sarah, who died over two years ago in a horrific car crash.   Sarah was like an older sister to me. Likewise, her sons and their families have become very precious to me for other reasons. I can't have children of my own because of a medical condition that was diagnosed when I was a teenager. At times I become depressed over the fact that I will never have children. My husband Marcus tells me all the time that I am enough, but I have doubts. Over the last few months, it's been hard to see my friends get married and have children. Oh, how I wish I had my own. After failed attempts to adopt and even foster children, my husband and I have resolved to live our life to the fullest, dedicating ourselves to Freedom Church. Yep, my Marcus is the pastor, and I am his wife.

      "Oh, it's not that bad. I've had an inspector come in and the house has solid bones. No structural problems. But it'll take a lot of sweat equity to get it operational by April," Nathan replies with a cute smirk. Nathan and Sofia are two of a kind. Sofia is a few months pregnant and glows, and he is over the moon in love. Young love has its perks. "Well, do we have a list of things that need to be done?" asks my new bestie Amy. Yep. Amy is Jared's new bride and while she is very different than Sarah, I've gotten close to her because I find her cool. She likes motorcycles and sometimes her mouth filter is off. My kind of friend. Since she married Jared, Amy has stepped forward to sing in the worship and praise band. Boy, what a voice! Her daughter Robin is not bad either. "Amy, we've got a list so we will sub out the electrical and plumbing, but we'll need to get some walls put up and some taken down. The plans have been approved by the city, so we'll need to keep the city inspector in the loop," Nathan replies with a wink at Sofia. *Good grief! Newlyweds everywhere!* Unlike the Moore family, Marcus and I have been married almost sixteen years, and it's been a great ride. I love Marcus and well... He's hot! Even more so than when he played football at the University of Canton. Linebackers have the best bodies. I hated him back then though. But back to the house.

As we walk through the house I notice a few things that need work as do the others also make suggestions for improvements. Nathan is typing down the information in his tablet. "I'll have Rocco come over later today and double-check behind me," Nathan told the group. Rocco's Nathan's flipping partner.

As we go through the house I'm walking beside Amy and notice her hair. The platinum blonde hair she had is gone! When I first met Amy last summer, she had platinum hair down to her shoulders. The length is the same but the color has changed back to what appears to be her natural look. "Amy? Great hair. New color?"

"No, Millie. This is my original color. I dyed it blonde to hide all my gray hairs. It's now a darker, more natural blonde. Jared said he doesn't care what color my hair is as long as I'm happy. If he didn't care then I guess that's good enough for me." She shrugs her shoulders. Good for her!

We finish the tour, getting all the information Nathan and Rocco need to compile a list, and then head out. We had the sign put up last week showing everyone what this new facility will be and how it will be used. The Mayor of Canton, the President of the University of Canton, and Jill McDaniels, my sister in Christ, the mother of my faith, another bestie, and President of the Board of Trustees at U of Canton are all on-board with this project. It's great to have friends in high places. It also helps that Jill is a fantastic attorney, and we solicit advice from her and her husband Cole constantly. As we leave, my Marcus pulls up, gets of out his car and waves at everyone. He comes up and puts his arm around my waist as I take in his luscious smells and his body is keeping me warm. Then after he whispers in my ear, "good morning" he further tells me, "You know it's going to snow again tonight, Millicent." Everyone else calls me Millie, and it seems odd, but my given name is like a pet name to Marcus. And it sounds sexy on his deep voice too. Is it hot in here?

"Yea, we should've stayed in the Caribbean," I tell everyone and we all laugh. Last month we all took a cruise together while Robin and her new husband, Greg, or Marshal Walker that is, were married. As we leave the house, I get in the car with Marcus. Of course, he opens the door for me like he has since we started dating. He's hot and I know I've mentioned that. When he gets in the driver's side of our car, he leans over and gives me a kiss on the lips, and whispers to me, "You know I love you, right?"

"What did you do?" I respond playfully. When he asks about love in a question he either has bad news or did something wrong. I'm guessing the latter. "Oh, nothing. I did get some news from social services. We are now on the list again for foster children, but nothing's come up yet."

"Then we'll leave it in God's hands," I reply and we

head home to avoid the impending snow. But my thoughts go to the loss I feel every time I'm reminded that I'm unable to have children.

****

The next day, we wake up to about five inches of snow on the ground. It's one of those days that we should stay in bed. I glance over at my husband, who made me feel like a queen last night. But we have to get out and start the day as it'll be a busy one. So, I get up, get my coffee and make my way to the living room with my journal and Bible in hand. This time of day is for me to have some alone time with the Lord. Today is no different, but in my prayers I feel that he's telling me to be prepared for tough times ahead. I can't shake that feeling! In a small snow event like today, while not enough to close school, it does create a little havoc. Plus it's Friday. I need to go by the mansion to check on the house, because for some reason I feel like we forgot to lock the door yesterday. Another thing in my quiet time is that there seems to be a compelling need I have in my heart to go to the Sarah Moore House. *I can't explain it.* I go back to the bedroom where Marcus had left to go to the study for his quiet time. I get ready, and after kissing my husband 'bye' I go outside and get in my car. Marcus will go to the hospital to visit a couple of patients that are church members. Usually Marcus has Friday off, but today is a busy day so he will probably take Monday off instead. I leave him in our house while he continues to go through his morning routine of Bible Study, quiet time, and getting ready for the day. I get in my old Honda Betsy that has 200,000 miles on it. But we take care of it and it is a great car. I drive down our street and look at Mavis' house as I pass by. Thinking back to a time that Mavis was a 'frenemy', she has become a Godsend to Charlotte and his family. That little Ellis is so cute! It makes me happy and sad at the same time that I'll never have a child like that. I don't know why but lately I've been reflecting on my relationship with my hottie husband Marcus and having children. I've known for a long time that I'm unable to have any, but I wish we could anyway. While driving to the mansion I remember the times Marcus and I've had together. We've been at Freedom Church for over ten years and prior we were at a church where Marcus was briefly an assistant pastor. And before that we knew each other in college. We hated each other. Marcus was, well...how should I put it...available to women. Yea, that's the best way to describe it. And to be truthful, I was the same way towards men, unfortunately. I know Marcus regrets his behavior and I regret mine. Marcus told me one time that he had one serious girlfriend that lasted a couple of months. But after that, he went crazy. Back then we were not Christians, but I came to Christ in my junior year when I got a new roommate. Yea - Jill. The same Jill that's my good friend. She led me to Christ. So I changed and Marcus, while we were never together in undergraduate, hated me for it. As a matter of fact he hated all Christians, until one day Dr. Porter changed his life, or in other words Jesus used. Dr. Porter to change Marcus' life. Dr. Porter is the current college president, but back then he was a professor who advised the campus ministry team called Infusion Exploration. In his senior year, Marcus injured his knee and well, his football career was over. A devastated Marcus had nowhere to turn and Dr. Porter was there to lead him to the Promised Land. After graduation he decided to go to seminary while I went to get my master's in counseling. After, I saw the change in him and it was attractive. Extremely attractive. So I did what any girl should do. I asked him out and the rest is history. We both graduated the same day and got married the next.

As I arrive at the mansion, I notice a light on in the front dining room that was not on yesterday. Hmm. I should call Marcus or the police but something tells me to go on in. I get out of my car and close the squeaky door. I really need to get that fixed. Slowly I step up to the door and listen for any sounds. Someone is... Sobbing? The door is unlocked, so I turn the doorknob and look in the entrance way. To my left is the old dining room. There I see a bundle of clothes moving. As I move forward the clothes move and I see a face looking at me. It's a girl or a young woman. Maybe thirteen or fourteen? The poor child has smelly clothes with holes in them and her face, while beautiful, is dirty. She's bundled up and is shivering. It is cold today, but fortunately, I had the power turned on last week so the heat's running at about fifty-five degrees. It's still cold inside. She peers up at me and immediately I'm heartbroken. Is she running away? If so from what? I step forward, not knowing what I'm getting into. I keep going then bend down to look closer. She's pale and needs help. After putting my hand on hers, I ask, "Can I help you?"

I get no answer. The poor child closes her eyes and becomes unresponsive. I know I'm in trouble now.

Chapter 2
Marcus

As usual, Millicent is gone before I am. She's my Warrior Queen. She's a no-nonsense person who always keeps me on my toes. I've been thinking about us and how the Caribbean trip was magical. She and I should have renewed our vows and I could kick myself for not thinking about it. But the trip was great not only for our friends but for us as well. I've long accepted the fact that we won't have kids and I know that was on Millicent's mind on the trip. Lately, Millicent seems to be more reflective and I think she's been thinking more and more about kids. But the Moore family is like our family. Since Millie and I came back to Canton over ten years ago, Jared and his family have been so open and welcoming to us. They've invited us on vacations and over for dinner many times. We've watch Nathan and Kyle grow into fine young Christian men, When Sarah died, it was devastating, but we asked Jared and his family to lean on us for support. That's what families do. I always craved a close knit family. I never knew my father and my mother died when I was in college of cancer. She did the best she could raising me, but without God in our lives, it was empty. It is so sad that she never knew Christ.

Millicent's life was worse. Her father was horrible to her mother and bolted when Millicent was young. As soon as her older sister, Willow, turned eighteen, she joined the military. While we've gotten postcards over the years, she's been silent for a long time, and we haven't been able to get in touch no matter how hard we've tried. National security and all. My understanding is that she's into secret military operations but I'm not sure. We haven't heard from her in

over ten years. That left Millicent to deal with her mother.
Her...uh...man-hating mother. She still hates me, but I can't
change her. Only God can. So we pray for her mother and
for the absent Willow. I have no other physical family,
except my church family and Millicent. I should be envious
of others, and while I'm tempted, I'm glad that many include
us in their lives. In addition to the Moore's, Jill and her
husband, Cole, along with their children Allison and Walt,
are also great friends. Cole is a great behind-the-scenes
attorney, but Jill is a dynamo. She's the face of The Law
Offices of *McDaniels, McDaniels, and Shannon.* Great TV
commercials. Allison and Walt are twins graduating from
high school this year. They help after school with running
the gym many of us go to, which is near the church. It's in
an old abandoned factory. Allison is a special child,
diagnosed with autism, and brilliant when it comes to math
and figures. She's memorized our church budget for the
year and also helps with some of the bookkeeping. Walt is
more of the athletic type and plays baseball for Canton
Academy. He will probably play at U of Canton next year
on a baseball scholarship. Jill led Millicent to Christ in
college. Then after their junior year, Jill and Cole got
married, then had the twins a year later. What they have
done with their lives is wonderful and a story to be shared.

     I try not to imagine what my life would be like if Dr.
Porter had not come along and saved me from a life of self-
destruction made of alcohol, pot, and women. No telling. In
reality, Jesus saved me. Dr. Porter was the seed planter.
Back in my freshman year, I was an eighteen-year-old punk.
I dated a girl back then for about three months. Breanna. I
thought back then she was "it" for me. But after three
months Breanna left me a note and disappeared without a

word. I tried to track her down but it was obvious that she was having some problems. Frankly, I was too. Pot, booze, and sex were all the rage. My life now could not have been predicted by my past behavior. But I'm grateful for the life I lead with my partner Millicent. I still don't know why a woman like her would even grace my presence, because she is not only the most beautiful woman I've ever seen, she's the smartest I know. When God gave out spiritual gifts, Millicent got in line four or five times. When God gave out beauty, she stayed in line until He gave her five helpings. That short, dark hair and piercing dark eyes can allure any man and I've noticed some look at her, and I get very protective. But Millicent can take care of herself. She's tall, slender and very athletic. And sexy. Yea, pastors can think their wives are sexy. I'm so glad she has eyes for only me. She is definitely a Proverbs 31 wife and I'm grateful every day for her.

     I finish getting ready to go to the hospital. I've had my daily prayer and meditation on the Word, but lately, the Lord is sending signals that we need to be prepared for something big. Millicent and I share about these things and I know she's getting the same vibe. What that is, is beyond either of us. Today though, I've got a few parishioners in the hospital, with one having bypass surgery today. One will probably die today. I don't look forward to that because Mr. Davis is such as nice fellow. This is not my favorite part of the pastor's role, as I hate hospitals. I was there when Sarah Moore died and it tore me apart. I've performed numerous funerals of people I know and people I don't know. That one I'll never get over. But I see now that out of the ashes God provides. And he has with the Moore family and those of us who knew and grieve for 'Saint Sarah'. She was one of a kind. As for Jared, he's remarried, and I'm still having a hard time believing it. His new wife, Amy, is still a big mystery to me, but Millicent has better insight into people sometimes and likes her a lot. The shelter project is great for Millicent, Amy and Amy's daughter, Robin, as they've experienced some form of abuse in the past. During our cruise last month, Robin got married to a great guy, Greg, who is a US Marshal and former military.

I'm finishing up and getting ready to leave our house, and as I pick up my cell phone it buzzes indicating a text message has arrived. Millicent texts me to come over to the mansion ASAP. So after quickly finishing up in the house I get in the car and leave our house. Passing Mavis' house I recall a few months ago how terrible that woman was and how she has been healed by Jesus. Her daughter Charlotte still has a long way to go but significant progress has been made. I need to get to the mansion and I still get somewhat concerned about my wife and her exploits. *What has she gotten into now? Lord, please help Millicent and please be with us.*

As I get closer to the house, I'm getting anxious. The closer I get, the more anxious I get. After ten minutes I arrive at the mansion to find an ambulance and Millicent standing next to it. Now, I'm about to freak out. I see Millicent standing outside next to the ambulance so I deduce now it's not her the ambulance is here for, but I still am very worried and in an almost panicked state. After cutting the ignition, I immediately jump out of the car not closing my door and yell "MILLICENT. ARE YOU OKAY?" I'm worried and out of my mind with concern because if something happened to her.... I run up to her and give her a hug. *Thank God she's safe.*

"Marcus, I'm fine but we had a visitor and well… she needs help. So I called an ambulance. We need to stay with her as I think she has nobody else." I nod my head and as the ambulance pulls away we get in my car and follow. While in the car, she explains about finding the girl, so I pull out my phone to call my young friend, Josie Bailey, who works at social services. She also attends Freedom Church. I have worked on several cases with Josie over these last five years since she graduated from U of Canton and started working for social services. Josie has been on my prayer list a while now. She's a believer, but I don't think she's moving forward with her life since she lost her fiance, Myron, several years ago. Now, she is in charge of her unit, a big step for a young person. "Josie, it's Marcus."

"Marcus. I assume this is not a social call or a church call. I was out-of-town Sunday and…"

"Josie it's not that. I have business for you. We found a girl at the shelter house, and we've called for an ambulance to take her to the hospital. She'll need someone from your office and... Josie... we don't know what we're dealing with here."

"Okay, Marcus. I'm at the hospital now on another case so I'll be meeting you in the lobby. It's Canton Central right?"

"Yes, that's right. See you in a minute." We hang up.

I turn to the love of my life who just scared five precious years of life out of me. "Are you okay?" I ask her as she's still shivering from the cold.

"Marcus I'm fine. But that poor baby. She's cold and..well...she passed out from something. She looked pale."

"It's going to be fine."

I pull out of the mansion driveway and make a way for the hospital. I carefully watch Millicent and see a tear go down her face. I never want my wife to cry or shed tears. In some way, it turns me into a protective beast. You mess with my wife, you mess with me. And I still have a linebacker mentality so maybe that's not a pastoral way of looking at things, but so be it. I would do anything for the love of my life. As I drive, Millicent is strangely quiet. Usually, she's a talker, and I am the opposite. This must have deeply affected my Millicent in a way that nothing else could. We've seen some bad stuff in our lives and this seems to be something different A few minutes later, I pull into the parking area for clergy and get out with Millicent by my side. I didn't have the time to open the door for her because she's darting towards the hospital entrance. As we get inside, Josie is waiting.

"Marcus. Millie. Sorry, we have to see each other again under these circumstances," Josie says as she looks up to us. She's short.

"Any news?" Millicent asks.

"Let's go on back. I've cleared it with the hospital." So we head back through the emergency waiting area to the room where they are examining the young lady. Yea, Millicent was right. She's skinny and pale. And, also dirty. I quickly glance at her clothes piled on the chair and they are dirty and...smelly. It's awful. I stand back taking it all in. Why do people treat others this way? I can tell right off the bat that this child has been abused or neglected or both. It took all of me to not show how angry I am at this moment. I want to tear someone's head off! I just don't know who. So

I go to the one person that will help me deal with these feelings and help this child. The Father, so I say a quick, silent prayer.

Dr. Alan Jacobson, who we know well and also goes to our church comes in to examine this mysterious child. Surprisingly he's a Messianic Jew, the only one, besides his family, in the congregation.
"Marcus...Millie...Josie..." says Alan. "We cannot seem to get any information out of her as she's refused to tell us her name. But I've drawn some blood. I believe she's got anemia and malnutrition. The test will confirm it. I can't seem to find anything else abnormal. I'd like to give her a tetanus shot and other immunizations at some point, as well as a physical examination. I don't find any bruises to suggest any signs of someone hitting or... other abuse. I also recommend that she gets cleaned up." Then Alan turns to the young lady and asks sympathetically, "I'm very sorry to ask you this but I have to ask. Has anyone...sexually assaulted you? Do you understand what I'm saying?" The young woman shakes her head 'no' emphatically and then stares at Millicent and me.

"Have you found a place to house her yet Josie?" Alan asks after a moment of silence. Josie gazes down at the floor, then before she responds, Millicent says, "We'll take her!." Before I could argue, Josie says to both of us, "Can we discuss this outside?" So we all go outside the room and Josie turns to us, then says, "Look. I know you both just got foster care re-certified, but are you sure you want to take this on? We know nothing right now and well... not knowing who she is can be...tricky."

"I don't care Josie. Make it happen," Millicent declares peering up at me as if I would say 'yes', which I would have without hesitation. The one thing about Millicent and me is that after being together we can almost read each other's mind. Go *Warrior Queen*! I nod my head affirming what my wife said and Josie pulls out her cell phone and steps away.

Chapter 3
Millie

As Josie walks away I wonder about our old friend now on her phone. Seeing Josie again though has made me worried about her. Josie is a beautiful young woman, but her life lately has taken its toll. She has auburn hair with dark green eyes and is what some people call a 'plain look'. Short too. About 5'2"? But she's haunted. I can tell because of the dark circles under her eyes, and the way she looks so not put together. At twenty-five, Josie appears more like a thirty-five-year-old. I'm hoping to get her out of her eight-year funk, but I can only handle what I can handle. And that leads to Marcus.

In all the years we've known each other Marcus has always called me "Millicent", which is my given name. Never "Millie", unless he's upset with me. And even then that's very rare. The man has the patience of Job, but I can tell that even this situation has taxed it. I believe he wants to pummel someone for neglecting this poor teenager. I feel sorry for the guy who gets in my husband's way when he's angry. Some quarterbacks did in college. A linebacker eats quarterbacks for lunch. Marcus affirming my statements to Josie is why I love him. Not that he's agreeable all the time, but when I'm right, I'm right. One thing about our marriage is that we rely on each other and trust each other's instincts one hundred percent. It's almost as if we read each other's minds. So while Josie goes into the corner to make phone calls, we wait in the hallway. Then Marcus tells me, "Since she's staying with us, we need to get the house in order. She can stay in the guest room for now, but she'll need clothes." So I text Sofia to let her know what I need from the Clothes Closet at church. She took my place as the preschool director January 1st, so she's at the church now, I assume. I get an emoji response of 'okay'. I hate emojis.

Anyway, we wait...and wait...and wait. As we continue to wait Marcus checks his phone for updates on email and parishioners, while I bite my nails, thinking about our new friend who has no name. Yep. I'm one of those nail-biters when I'm nervous. We continue to wait...and wait in what seems like forever then Alan comes out, while at the same time Josie gets off the phone and headed towards us. Alan says, "Okay, we gave her a shot to help with the anemia, but when she gets to a place, have her intake food very slowly and she needs plenty of water. I'm also prescribing some special vitamins, some antibiotics for a few days just in case, and we just removed the IV. She'll need clothes so I asked the gift shop downstairs to provide scrubs. That'll do until she gets to..?" He peers at Josie and she says, "She's going with the M&M gang here."

"Yes," I reply with a chuckle.

"Okay. Well, as long as she gets somewhere comfortable." And, then Alan smiles and goes back into the room.

"Marcus? Millie? I've been in touch with the appropriate people and she's in your emergency care for now but we'll need to do some legwork later and get the court involved. We need to get her to your house. But we also need to find out who she is, so if you do please let me know. I feel that if there are other children in that house like her, we're in trouble." Josie seems very concerned and I hadn't thought about that but it makes sense. I don't know why I'm drawn to this child. She reminds me of me a long time ago I guess. My mother did not take care of us, and when my sister Willow left it was worse. Even though she says she hates men, they came and went like a revolving door. My old ways mirrored her ways. I've tried to help my mother but now she even refuses to talk to me. That was when Marcus and I got married. I still call but she refuses to even acknowledge me. *Maybe God knew I'd be a bad parent. Is that why I never had children? I'll never know.*

A few minutes later, Alan comes out again and tells us she's good to go. We then go inside the hospital room. Josie tells our new ward, "Honey, you're safe. Can you tell me your name?" She opens her eyes towards me with those doe eyes of hers. They're light brown, matching her long, greasy light brown hair. Her hair goes to her waist and it seems that it has never been cut or anything. She's going to be tall as I'm 5'10" and she's only a couple of inches shorter than me. Beautiful child. She motions for me to come closer and I do. Then she whispers her name in my ear. "Angel," she says. "What a pretty name," I respond with a smile. "Can I tell the others?" I ask. She nods and I tell Marcus and Josie her name is "Angel".

I look right at her and tell her, "Angel you're very pretty. Can you tell me your last name?" She shakes her head 'no' and I left it alone for now. "Are you hungry? How about we get something to eat. The doctor says we can go and I'll fix you something light. Doctor's orders." I hand Marcus the prescriptions to fill at the pharmacy later. She then gets up and holds my hand.

Fortunately, the hospital had shoes and scrubs her size. Coats they did not have so I give Angel mine. I'll bet Alan paid for the stuff. He's like that. Then the nurse comes in and we sign her papers to check out. A nursing assistant brings a wheelchair and we start down the hall. Marcus goes on ahead to get the car to pull around. As we get to the entrance, Josie leans over to tell me, "You made progress, but we have a ways to go. Find out what you can." I nod and we walk out to the waiting car. Josie gets ready to leave by giving me a side hug, as she departs, Angel waves and gives a slight grin then we get in the car. With her having my coat I do notice the cold air and light snow coming down. Boy, I wish we were in the Bahamas.

****

In a few minutes, we pull in our driveway. As we pull up we see Mavis in her car waiting for us. She probably was volunteering at the Church in her grandson's nursery room when I texted Sofia earlier. I get out as she does and Mavis reaches in her back seat to pull out a box. Marcus runs over and tells Mavis, "Please, let me get that. I don't want you to hurt yourself, Mavis."

"Thanks, Marcus," Mavis replies. Now, Mavis would have barely talked to either one of us a few months ago, nor made any effort to help anyone out. She was a recluse. With her reconnecting with her daughter Charlotte, she has come out of her shell. Too bad my mama can't.

As Marcus takes the box inside, I go around to help a weak Angel out of the car, with Mavis also guiding her. Mavis leans over to Angel and tells her, "These people are the best child. They'll take care of you and we'll help." *Who is this person and what did she do with the old Mavis?* So we go inside where it's warm and cozy. Now our house is nice because both Marcus and I work on it to be nice. We're pretty handy around the house and while we don't make a lot of money, it is a nice place to live. Nathan has come over to help with a few projects. He's got a home flipper side hobby and works with a contractor who goes to our church. His name is Rocco. But I digress. The neighborhood is not bad, but not good either. Marcus has taken the box to the guest room and the rest of us are seated at the kitchen island.

"Okay Angel how about soup for an afternoon lunch and grilled cheese. Mavis, you want coffee?"

"No thanks. I want to head back to the church so I can get more of my Ellis fix," Mavis replies. Ellis is her grandson. Now I know why she's in a giddy mood. So I walk her to the door, and she leans over and says, "Millie, if you need anything let us know." Then she leaves.

Coming back in the kitchen I see Marcus sitting at the island glancing at his watch. I know he needs to get back to the hospital so I say, "Marcus we're fine here. Why don't you leave and come back for supper? There's no meeting at the church tonight so we can get acquainted with each other. Also, don't forget the prescriptions for Angel." I want Angel alone to try and find out more about her. Just then, Angel trembles, then gazes back up and is all of a sudden appears scared. Then she says in a shaky voice, "Marcus should stay here. Marcus should stay so we'll be safe!"

Marcus leans over to Angel who is trembling with fear, and calmly tells her, "You're safe with Millicent. While she fixes your lunch, how about I show you your room and some other things." So I turn to fix tomato soup and grilled cheese. My go-to favorite.

Chapter 4
Marcus

I am surprised that Angel even wants to be near me. Usually, a female child wants to be near another female when traumatized, but this is unusual and unnerving. I take her back to the office and show Angel the display case with trophies in it hoping it gives her a sense of calm. "Angel, do you see these trophies?" She nods her head. "Millicent is a black belt in Karate and even teaches women self-defense at the church on Tuesdays. It's called the *Mama Bear Self-Defense.* She also packs a gun for protection and is very proficient. So I feel like you are safe with her. Others need me to help them." Angel puts her hand in mine and nods, then smiles a bit. So far, so good. Then we get to the guest room. I put her things down on the bed. "Angel, when you get a chance, have Millicent get you to try these things on and if you need anything else, let us know, okay?" She again nods without saying anything then reaches to hug me. I almost lose it there because while we know we will never have children, I feel a connection with this girl. She's almost as tall as Millicent but really skinny, so I have to be gentle in my hugs. If I'm not careful I could break her like a pretzel. I'm a big guy and still a linebacker at heart. Then she releases me, and we return to the kitchen and sit at the island while I watch my lovely, sexy wife finish up lunch. Then she serves all of us. I then hold Angel's hand and Millicent holds her other hand forming a circle while I begin the prayer.

Father, thank you for sending Angel to us and thank you for today. Bless this food to our bodies and keep us healthy and safe. In Jesus' name. Amen.

"Why do you pray and who do you pray to?" asks Angel. Now here is the opportunity that all believers should have. To witness to a person. Focusing on her while we eat, I say to her, "We pray to give thanks to our Heavenly Father who is God. Jesus is God's Son and gave his life for us so we can have eternal life. Do you understand what I'm saying, Angel?"

"Not really. My mother prayed some, but we never went to church or anything. She did pray at the end though." Angel continued to eat as Millicent and I stare at each other quizzically. What does 'the end' mean? By Millicent's facial expression, I know she's thinking the same thing I am. As we eat I quickly glance at my watch and know I have to go so I get up and go over to kiss Millicent and tell her "I love you." Then I go and hug Angel. She says, "Marcus. Do you love me?" At that my heart breaks. This child needs us and needs love in her life. We don't know what happened to her but we have to know and soon. I feel like that she's in very serious trouble.

"Angel. I do love you and so does Millicent. You are safe here and can tell us anything." Angel returns to her lunch eating it very slowly. I lean over and hug her again and go to Millicent and give her a not-so-romantic kiss on the check, though I wish it was more. Then I grab my keys and leave.

I get out of the driveway and head up the street towards Cleveland Avenue. As I drive towards the hospital I use my car system to call Josie. "Josie, it's Marcus."

"Marcus. Any news yet?"

"Well, she said something peculiar a minute ago. She said her mother prayed at the end. I can only take that as being that she died."

"Yea. That helps. We quickly researched all the state school records and could not initially find her existence, but with so little information it's like looking for a needle in a haystack. So I'm trying to find out anything from the nearby Pennsylvania schools and now I'll look into recent deaths, but I just got off the phone with Detective Lt. Sandra Coblentz to open a case with the Canton PD. You know Sandra right?"

"Yes, Sandra and I have run into each other before, and she goes to the second service when she's not on duty."

"Marcus, my other line is beeping. Can I can you back?"

"Let me call you later Josie. I'm headed back to the hospital and my phone just beeped too." We hang up. As I continue to drive I think about the events of the day. Angel is a mystery. A puzzle that needs to be solved. Maybe Millicent will have some good fortune today. I pull up at the hospital for the second time today and check my phone which gives me a weather alert for snow tonight. Big deal. It snows all the time here. This is northeast Ohio, not Florida. So I get out of my car and head into the entrance.

As I enter the hospital I want to go through the therapy waiting room as it's a shortcut to the area of the hospital for Mr. Davis's room. Mr. Davis will soon pass away today from cancer. The family should've called hospice as I advised, but that's an argument for another day. While Mr. Davis is a good and Godly man, his family is something else. As I enter the therapy waiting room I see Amy and Jared there. I wave 'hello', but Jared and Amy appear as they've been in an argument or heated discussion of some kind. I guess the honeymoon's over.

Anyway, I come over and greet them. "What do you say, Jared. Amy. What brings you here?"

Jared replies with a frustrated voice, "Marcus? Sarah's younger brother Nick is here. He arrived earlier this week from Walter Reed to finish rehab from a battle injury to the shoulder. then he will be officially discharged from the Army. He's going to stay at the farm's bunkhouse temporarily. And we want to drop by and see Jenny, Nick's aunt before we leave." Now I know what the argument's about. Amy is a little sensitive about Jared's previous wife. I can understand. 'Saint Sarah' looms large in the community still after all of these years.

I tell both of them, "Well that's wonderful. Let me know when I can visit with him. But I have to get upstairs and start my visits. Mr. Davis will probably pass if he's not already done so, so I need to go. I'll see you later?" I wave and move on to the elevators. It's going to be a long day.

****

After spending a few hours at the hospital I'm dragging to the car. My good friend and Godly brother Alvin Davis did pass away and I had two others to see, including Jenny Akers who's battling a serious case of the flu and dehydration. Jenny was Sarah's aunt so I guess she's Nick's too. But, I take solace in the fact that Alvin's in a better place now. Mr. Davis was a good man who gave of himself. He was wealthy I think, but used it in ways that I don't even know. I know he paid for someone to go to school as he asked me to deliver an envelope to the financial aid office at the University of Canton two weeks ago. I don't know what it was all about but I complied with his wishes. Not my business.

I also heard that Old Man Brown was brought in and died of a heart attack. Dr. Brown was not a member of the church or a believer as far as I know. But he was the Provost at the U of Canton for a long time. A... Very... Long... Time. As the chief academic officer, he hired faculty and initiated academic programs. I tried to get some of the seminary classes moved to the church last year and help get more interns, but he refused. I thought a more practical setting was in order and I had the support of just about everybody but Dr. Brown blocked it. I'm not sure what hold he had on the University's leaders, but he did. Now Dr. Brown is gone. Where? I do not know.

I go to the hospital pharmacy to pick up Angel's prescriptions. I also stop by the PT department but Jared's brother-in-law had already left as well as Jared and Amy. Back to Mr. Davis. The poor man wasn't even dead for five minutes before the family was arguing about money, the house, and even his 22-year-old granddaughter, Morgan, was trying to get a little too close to me. I hate that. It's happened before with other women. Because of my dark past, Millicent and I made a commitment to tell each other everything as we are mutually accountable to one another. That is not a conversation I want to have tonight, particular with a guest in the house. I can still smell that sickly perfume on me that Morgan had on! What is it - *la mauvaise odeur* (That is a rough French translation for bad smell or *pee-yew* I think)? My French is rusty as I only had a semester of it in college and I slept through it most of the time. As I pull out of the hospital parking lot it's almost six and dark. Before I leave I text Millicent that I'm on my way, then I turn on the radio to hear the city's favorite band,

Melting Squash, and its latest hit, "Love is Like Tomato Soup". The lead singer attended Freedom Church with Nathan when he was in school. David Salley and I have a special friendship and we correspond by email when he's on the road. I wish he would use his talent for God's glory and not just for entertainment, but God will work that out. I have a feeling he already is doing something in David's life. The band is pretty good though. I'm a jazz fan myself while Millicent is a hard rocker. As I pull the SUV out, my mind wanders to our mysterious guest in the house. *Who is Angel? What's the backstory here? Is she or we in danger?* Good questions with no answers.

After a few minutes of fighting traffic, snow, and cold, I pull in our driveway and stop the car. I put it in park, take a long breath and pray again that God will help us through this mystery. Yet I have a feeling that God has sent this child to us for a reason and he's not done yet. As a pastor, I counsel many people to have joy even in tough times, but sometimes that's been easier said than done. I just feel uneasy about the future as if a seismic change is coming for Millicent and me. I can't put my finger on it though. I get out of the car and head towards the house, then open the front door to find supper on the table and Angel setting the places. So far, so good at the house even though we are having salad. Yuk! I was hoping for a steak or something with meat. Millicent has been on a health kick lately. We both turn forty this year and she thinks we're over-the-hill. As I call out to Millicent, Angel jogs to the door and greets me with a hug. I receive it and look over at Millicent, who's simultaneously watching me from the kitchen island.

"Angel. Did you have a good day?"

"Uh Huh. Marcus. Thanks for asking. The chicken for the salads is still cooking so it won't be long. I helped and everything!" A little excitable now. Huh?

Millicent comes over and I release Angel and lean towards my wife to give her a kiss on the lips and a hug. She smells a lot better than that Davis child. Millicent is like a spring morning. Always smells like flowers and an ocean breeze.

"Marcus. Angel was very helpful today. Why don't you go change and I'll be there in a minute. Angel? Would you monitor the chicken in the oven while Marcus and I get settled a bit," Millicent says with a slight smile towards Angel. Angel nods her head, smiles, and goes in the kitchen, while I head towards our bedroom. Now, our bedroom is downstairs while the others are upstairs as well as our shared office. I get in our bedroom and lay down on the bed with my face in my pillow. It's that bad.

"Who was she?" Millicent asks. I know she smelled that icky stuff on me.

"Mr. Davis' overly affectionate granddaughter Morgan. You know her." I chuckle as I feel Millicent enter the room and close the door. "By the way, Mr. Davis passed this afternoon," I add.

I turn over and Millicent is hungrily watching me. Man, she's beautiful. What did I do to deserve her? "We made progress today," Millicent says.

Chapter 5
Millie

Today was wild to say the least. After we got back here, the first thing Angel did was to take a shower. In a word she reeked. So we went in the upstairs bathroom where I showed her where the towels and everything is located. I also got her some of my Amish-made shampoo and body wash. I like it because it has tea tree oil and Vitamin E. Good for the skin and hair. Also none of that factory goop they use now. All natural and with a hint of flower scent. Marcus likes that. I left the room to go into her bedroom to lay out some clothes. Her bedroom. Sounds permanent. About ten minutes later, Angel comes in the bedroom with a towel wrapped around her. She appears 100% better. So, Angel and I decide to get her room in order, so we go through the stuff Mavis brought from the church. She tries on every stitch of clothing and they all fit and look good. But the items lack some personal things like underwear, and...well... female stuff she'll probably need. So when we get some warm clothes on we leave the house. We then get into my old, trusty Betsy and go to the store to get her some undies, more age appropriate sleepwear, and toiletries. She tells me, almost embarrassingly, that her period is approaching so we got her items for that too. Then we come back. Throughout the afternoon I rack my brain to figure out what I could do to draw more information about who she is and where she's from. In the car, I tried to engage in conversation but nothing worked. She just smiled and nodded. But her smiles appear pasted on and fake. So far, she has said very little and looks very sad. Frustrated, I try to figure out

ways to get her to talk. So when we get back home I ask
her to put her stuff away and help me get ready for dinner.
She seems eager to help. Then it hit me. Maybe that's the
answer. She's a helper at heart. Maybe she's had to take
care of someone in her past. I sit down at the kitchen island
and notice my blank calendar sitting on the counter, which I
had not filled out yet with birthdays, anniversaries, and other
things. I know. Old school. So an idea formed. I sat at the
island and opened the calendar up. The calendar has some
pictures of some cute animals but that's not important right
now. As I sit down, Angel comes back down the stairs and
into the kitchen. As my thoughts have reflected on the day
so far I'm brought back to the reality of now. Now is time
where I either get her to talk or we go back to square one.

"What can I do to help?" Angel asks excitedly. I
just didn't have the heart to tell her we're having baked
chicken salad tonight. I've been on a health kick and my
cooking skills stink. And that's putting it mildly.

"Angel, honey, take out the chicken breasts out of
the bag in the sink, and place each breast on the baking
pan that's underneath the stove." She complies
wholeheartedly. "And wash your hands." I wish I was more
enthusiastic about cooking but I try not to show my
disinterest. "The chicken is already seasoned so put it in
the pan and set the oven for 350 degrees. Can you do
that?"

"Yes ma'am," she replies. *I'm too young for
'ma'am', right?* She's still smiling. Who knew chicken could
be this exciting? I really need to get Sofia to cook us
something. I immediately realize that Angel has the gift of
service. Therefore I need to exploit that angle to get more
information. I ask Angel to come over to the island and help

me with the calendar after I instruct her to wash her hands again. *No germs!* She does what I say without question. I bet most parents don't have it this good, so far.

So I go into my calendar job. "Okay. Angel. I need to complete this calendar for the year and my writing is terrible. Can you write well?" It really is terrible.

"I got an 'A' in English last year," Angel tells me. Clue number one. She went to school.

"Was that eighth grade English? Do they still teach writing? I'm curious about what schools teach these days because I used to be the preschool director at church and the field interests me," I cleverly say.

"Yea. The teacher was very strict at...our school." Angel almost gives something away and stops herself, but I have another clue. She was in eighth grade last year so that means she may be fourteen.

I turn to the calendar and flip to January, then February. I turn to Angel and instruct her, "Now write 'Marcus' Birthday' on February 19th. That's his birthday." She writes it down and then turns to me and asks, "What do you usually get him?"

"Well. Last year, I got him a new winter hat, but he never wears it. So maybe we can go get him something soon. We spend more money going out on Valentine's Day so we try to limit what we spend on birthdays. But he turns 40 this year, like me, so we need to get something extra special."

"Millie. Will I be here for that long?" Angel asks with a hint of sadness in her voice. Good question.

"Good question. I sincerely hope so. Angel? Marcus and I care about you and want to help you any way we can. Let's put that question in God's hands for now.

Okay?" I hope my answer gets her thinking about staying, and maybe about God. I wouldn't mind, but as I told her, that's the Lord's job. We just need to pray about it. So I tell Angel, "Let's pray now about it." And we do.

Lord, you know what's best for Angel but we come today with a special request that Angel stay with us long-term. But whatever your will is we'll be satisfied. Amen.

As we get through to May, I tell her to mark May 22nd as our anniversary. She hesitates, then looks down at the calendar again. She marks it in small letters for that day. I ask the obvious question, "Why the small letters?"

"That's also my birthday," Angel whispers. So I tell her to write it in so she smiles and does just that. Another mystery solved. We get through June, July, and August listing Willow's birthday and my mom's, and when we reach September, she stops and a tear comes from her left eye. "Is there someone who has a birthday in September you want to mark?" I ask her. Angel peers straight at me and tears are forming in both of them now. She points to September 15th and chokes up. Then she says, "My mother's birthday was that day." I'm very sad for this child, but we have another clue. Her mother is deceased I believe and her birthday is that day. So I hug her and after a moment she wipes her tears away, and I tell her, "We'll remember her so put it down and I promise will do something to remind us of how special she was." So she writes it down.

After finishing the calendar, I hang it up and take down last year's calendar and throw it away.

We sit a few minutes and I feel led in my heart to tell Angel my story. "Angel? You're fortunate to have a mother that loved you. My mother hates me to this day or acts like it. I'm fortunate to be here today myself. I didn't handle my mother's rejection very well and acted out by being with other boys and stuff. I also did a lot of other things I'm not proud of. It wasn't until I found Jesus that I had the strength to forgive my mother and to let go of my guilt for my behavior. And, even though my mother has nothing to do with me, I've tried to be forgiving and move forward in my life. God gave me Marcus, my friends and now you. And, God has sent you here to be with us. For how long, we do not know, but you will always have a place here."

Angel peered at me with wide eyes and a small tear again goes down her check. She gets up from her seat and comes over to me and gives me a hug. Then she tells me, "I hope I can stay here for a long time." I watch her carefully and tears form in my eyes. I've fallen in love with this child and I can't think of any way to avoid that. *Can you bond with a child after a few hours?* I guess natural parents do. If she is taken from us now my heart would be broken to bits. We release each other and I tell her to check on the chicken. She comes back and sits for a moment, then I tell her, "Angel. Tomorrow would you like for me to do your hair. I want to style it a bit, then we can go get a couple of nice things at the thrift store for church on Sunday. Sunday we will leave early for church then maybe go somewhere to eat. We seem to get lunch invitations all the time." Angel eyes me and genuinely smiles. "I'd like that. Maybe you and Marcus can tell me more about Jesus."

"I think that can be arranged," I reply, very happy how today has gone. We have a long way to go but so far, so good. I glance at my watch and then my phone pings. Marcus has texted me that he's on his way from the hospital.

A few minutes later I notice it's dark outside even though it's still early, and Marcus has just come in. He looks like he's been through the wringer. Mr. Davis must've died.

Chapter 6
Marcus

"So how much progress?" I ask Millicent as I still lay on the bed next to her. "Well, we got her age, birthday, mother's birthday, and some other tidbits that Josie and Sandra can use." Millicent is a genius and very gifted. She should've been a detective. Millicent continues on and tells me, "Her birthday is the same day as our anniversary." Now as a pastor I don't believe in coincidences. Maybe this is divine intervention. We'll just have to see. I change the subject to the one that is twisting me inside right now.

"Millicent? That granddaughter needs a filter and some self-control. Maybe get her to go to the single women's retreat or something. But the family is worse. They kept arguing about money and themselves. Mr. Davis wasn't even cold yet! I thought a fight would break out. It was depressing and ridiculous. I'm going to hate doing the funeral. Maybe they'll ask somebody else?" I don't think so. I know Mr. Davis had all of the arrangements planned out for his family and probably anticipated the family discord. I know he did based on my previous conversations with him. He lived a full life and is now with Jesus so while I'm sad about a pillar of the church passing to glory, I'm happy that he doesn't suffer anymore. He's even picked out the hymns to be sung at the event. I'm willing to bet a packed house of local dignitaries. I think he let it slip that he redid his will a few months ago, but that's not my business.

Millicent grabs my arm trying to drag me from the bed. Oh, how I wish we could stay here. "Marcus. Get more comfortable, then come join us for dinner. Please compliment Angel about helping me. I think I've figured her out a bit. She's a service-oriented person, and we need to encourage that aspect right now. And, we're going to get some more stuff for her tomorrow, and she'll need to register for school soon. We have a long way to go." Millicent gives me a sexy kiss on my lips and I feel the same electrical current I've felt ever since I kissed her the first time many years ago. Then my beautiful bride whispers to me, "I love you Marcus, and I always will... Before you come in, wash that stench off of you." I'm so blessed to have her in my life and I'm finding that Angel is a blessing too.

Millicent leaves the room. So I get up and change into my lounge pants and a t-shirt. Now about t-shirts. I collect them. And, I do wear one every Sunday to church with a pair of jeans and a sports coat. I know that's not traditional, but who cares. I do it to make a point that it doesn't matter how we dress for church. It's about Jesus, and he accepts us as we are. So Sunday I'll be wearing my Martin Luther King, Jr., shirt in honor of the man's birthday. I admire him and even wrote my master's thesis on his writings and theology. I was fascinated in seminary with his letters from the Birmingham jail. But tonight I pick out one of my superhero shirts.

I go out into the kitchen area where everything is set for dinner. Angel and Millicent are sitting at the island waiting for me. As I sit down I'm reminded of what we're having. Baked chicken and salad. Yuk! Again I wish we had some meat like a steak or something. But I don't complain. Millicent has many talents but cooking is not one of them. Maybe we could get Sofia or Nathan to make us something? Hmm. I glance up to see Angel and Millicent waiting on me for the prayer. So I say the blessing thanking the Lord for our food, but secretly wishing for steak. We all say 'Amen' at the end. What I've noticed when I look at Angel is a more openness towards Jesus and she seems happier. And, clean. And well... nice. Her hair needs some styling but she's a lovely young woman. I'd be happy for her to be our new daughter, but I can't get ahead of myself. However, it's like we have our own family unit here. We generally eat in comfortable silence and when I finish I wait for the others to finish. I'm a fast eater. So I open a conversation saying, "Angel. Thanks for helping with dinner tonight. It was... delicious... and I know you've had a full day. Is there anything you would like to do this evening?"

"Well. I can clean up and do laundry, and clean the bathroom and do anything you want and..."

"Whoa, Angel. Hold your horses," I interrupt. "Listen. You can contribute to the family here by doing some chores but you don't have to do everything. We need to have something to do."

Angel stares down at the floor and tells us, "I'm sorry. I just had to do everything back home because my mom couldn't. She was..." She stops then Millicent responds, "It's okay honey. But Marcus is right. Why don't we sit down and create a chore schedule for all of us? Marcus and I have our chores so we just need to adjust some things based on what our strengths are. By the way, I need to make more laundry detergent."

"Can you cook?" I blurt out. Oops. I was thinking that but really should not have said that out loud. Millicent hits me on the shoulder and we all laugh. Well, Millicent and I laugh. Angel appears confused, then declares proudly, "I can cook some, but we didn't have much food in our apartment." Well got another clue there. She lived in an apartment.

"Honey. I know we look forward to tasting your cooking. Maybe when we go to the thrift store tomorrow for church clothes, afterward we can go to the grocery store and pick up some things you like and you can tell me what you can cook then. And you could teach me. Or we can get my friend Sofia to help us." I like that idea. Just then a knock comes from the front door.

"I'll get it," Angel says. But I stop her by putting my hand up gently on her shoulder, and protectively instruct, "No. Angel. Let me this time." So she sits back down and I go to the door. I look through the peephole because I want Angel to make sure to do that when she's here, then notice that Greg Walker and his stepson Jesse are at the door. Greg is a US Marshal assigned to the Canton area and is Robin's husband. Robin is Amy's daughter from a prior marriage and Jesse's mother. The Moore family tree is a tough one to draw but they are a family that has been tested and come through the dark times and the good times over the last few years and even recently. Greg just took down a notorious criminal a few months ago.

I unlock the door and see them standing there. "Greg. Jesse. Come on in. We're just finishing supper." I say this and hear dishes clinging together in the kitchen. Angel must be putting them in the dishwasher. Good girl. They come in and Greg responds, "Marcus. Sorry for the interruption but we wanted to check in on Angel and see how's it going. Sandra called me earlier to talk about the case and I asked my friend Deek from the FBI to help us with any federal resources. And, I wanted to have Angel meet Jesse as they may be near in age. Everyone needs a friend."

My daddy protection mode kicks in as I'm not so sure I want a guy meeting Angel yet. But Jesse has proven in the short time I've known him to be a gentleman and a good guy, for a young teenage boy. As we enter Angel and Millicent appear out of the kitchen and I offer everyone a seat in the living room. Jesse goes up to Angel and introduces himself. "Hi, Angel. I'm Jesse." He sticks his hand out though I can tell he's checking her out. And Angel's checking him out too. Hmm. I don't know about this. Angel shakes his hand and we all sit in the living room with Jesse maneuvering to sit next to Angel. At least he's keeping a little distance. Angel seems to not be fearful of him though. Maybe Jesse could find out more about Angel. *We need a home location and her mother's name!*

"So Greg? How's the new job?" Millicent asks.

"It's great. Not too stressful yet, but I have to fly out to Arizona next week to get a prisoner that's being extradited back here. It won't be a tourist trip but at least it'll be warm for a little bit." Millicent offers everyone coffee or other beverage and Greg and I accept. "Angel? I fixed the coffee and it's ready. Would you get some for all three of us and anything for you and Jesse?"

"Yes ma'am," Angel replies and gets up. Jesse immediately jumps up and tells everyone, "I'll go help." I'm really gonna have to watch this. Not. Happy. At. All. Greg snickers and leans over to tell me, "You're gonna need a baseball bat to beat all the guys who even look at her."

"I'll just use my hands. I don't need weapons. And you're right. She will draw in the boys and Jesse's just the beginning. But we need to know more about her. We have some information so far. When you leave tonight, talk to Jesse to see if she opens up to him. I feel like we're running out of time," I tell Greg after the teens leave for the kitchen. And in this situation, time is not our friend.

****

That night we get Angel settled for bed. She seems comfortable. *Is this the only bed she's slept in?* So many questions. As we get in our room, I glance at Millicent and can tell she's exhausted. No fun tonight. Well, I'm tired too. So after doing our routines in the bathroom, we go to bed.

About midnight, I hear a couple of noises coming from upstairs. I lean over at Millicent and before I try to awaken her, she sits up and says, "I hear it too. Let's find out what it is." So we get up and head upstairs to where Angel's sleeping. As we get closer to the door we hear Angel talking.

"Please. Mom? Are you okay? Mom? Please don't hurt me Big Daddy. Please? AHHHHHHHHHHHHHHHHHHHHHHHH!" As she yells Millicent goes to her and shakes Angel. "Angel wake up! It's Millie. It's only a dream."

Angel wakes up sweating and shaking from the horrific nightmare. She sits up and confusingly puts her eyes on Millicent then me. Then she leans into her as Millicent is sitting on the bed now. And then Angel starts sobbing. Millicent hugs her, tells her it's okay and encourages Angel to go back to sleep. As we leave her room, Millicent leans over to me and asks, "Who's Big Daddy?" Another question with no answer. Perhaps the police will know more with this new revelation.

Chapter 7
Martin Luther King Holiday Weekend
Millie

Today is Sunday. My favorite day of the week. Angel and I spent yesterday at the thrift store and the grocery store. I found out that Angel has been cooking for her and her mother for years, and she has no siblings. I then gave all of the information in an email to Josie and Sandra yesterday when we got home when I had some privacy. After he went to the gym, Marcus cleaned up around the house, did laundry, and when we got back, Angel made us a spaghetti dinner. She can cook pretty well. Yep. I'm going to enlist Sofia to teach some things to both of us. The clothes Angel picked out for Sunday were very appropriate and with some guidance, we applied a little makeup. Angel doesn't need much, just a little. I also use natural makeup and encourage Angel to do so. Yea, some consider me a 'granola cruncher', but really I just try to live a thrifty life. Some things can be made cheaper, like laundry detergent, than being bought at the store. Back to church. Jesse greets us today and I think he likes Angel, but right now Angel needs to take care of herself and we need to solve this mystery. *Who is she?* We're slowly peeling the onion and we should have enough for Sandra and Josie to do their job.

As we sit in the front row, like I usually do, Angel attracts stares from many people, curious about the new person in our lives. It's the fishbowl effect of being a pastor's family. I've also found that Angel doesn't like unwarranted attention, but is very helpful in volunteering to pass out bulletins. Freedom Church has two services and today we decide to sit through both. I want to give Angel an idea of what worship can be. The first service is a light contemporary service, while the second service is what Marcus calls the "rock-n-roll Jesus" service. Robin and Amy sing with the worship team, while Jesse and Nathan are in the booth running sound. Jared reads the scripture passage today. As the sounds of music fade and the offering plates have been passed, the love of my life gets up to speak.

"Friends we call ourselves Freedom Church for a reason. In today's lesson in Galatians 5:13-14, Paul talks amount Freedom and liberty. In today's society, people make big talk about being free to do what they want, but is that freedom? No! Freedom is not supposed to abused by living a sinful life. And what is a sinful life? The church is struggling with that issue today. But the Bible is clear what sin is. And being a slave to sin is not really freedom at all. God gives us the freedom to choose. We can choose to live for ourselves. Satisfy our desires. Our wants. Our own flesh. Or, we can choose to serve others. Put God first and then others. What a radical concept. We choose a church because of what it can do for me. But what about choosing a church for how you can serve others. How about a job. How many of us choose jobs based on money and not based on serving others. Or a house or a car. Where are your priorities in life? Freedom is the assurance of knowing the final outcome of it all. That God takes care of us, even if we go through tough times. Who do you turn to during times of trial? Others? Well, unfortunately, none of us are completely reliable. But God is. Jesus is. Jesus is enough for all of us, regardless of what we've done."

In his MLK t-shirt, Marcus looks really good. I

glance over at Angel who's sitting to my left and a tear is coming down her face. She's convicted. I know it. I really hope we're getting through. Marcus takes a sip of water and with his Bible in hand, he comes out of the podium area and is now on the floor of the auditorium in front of the 500 people attending this service. Then he continues.

"I counsel couples who are breaking up and when they start saying 'I'm just not happy' or 'I've had enough' I point out that the focus should not be on the 'I' or the 'me' but on the other person. I know that's too simple for some relationships, but let me ask a question. Would there be world peace, would we have better government, a better life if everyone focused on others and not themselves? Maybe we should think about freedom in Christ as being focused on the freedom to help others. If we love ourselves should we not love others? Friends. I have lived a selfish life in the past. I've made no secret of my past and I'm telling you that it lead me to an empty life. A life without purpose. While fulfilling my temporary wants of self-medication led to temporary happiness, it did not lead to joy. In Ecclesiastes, Solomon calls the empty pursuits of life a chasing of the wind. And he was right. You see, happiness for self is temporary, but joy in Jesus is permanent. If you want that joy, then at the end of the service come down on the last song and I'll be here along with others on the staff."

As the last song is being sung I'm moved to prayer and as I'm praying for God to move the lost, I feel movement next to me. I quickly peer up as Angel is making her way to the front. As she reaches there, Marcus hugs her and says, "Welcome to Jesus my sister." We may not know who she is but God does, and now she's a true part of us. *The beginnings of a family?*

As the song continues to play, Marcus greets others and when the last verse is being sung a young man comes forward. He looks vaguely familiar but I can't determine whether I've seen him before or not. He has somewhat lighter skin than Marcus, and is slightly shorter but has an athletic build. Football player? Maybe. In seeing the two side by side they appear similar, yet, while Marcus is a joyful individual, the younger man is angry, and that anger exudes from his demeanor. He leans over and asks Marcus "Can I see you in your office after service?" Marcus points to me and I know from that it means that I need to be in his office with him, therefore, I'll need to do something with Angel. She has returned next to me since I'm on the front row near where Marcus is standing. I ask Angel, "Do you mind going to ask Jared and Amy if you could go home with them for lunch. Their family will probably be there and you can talk to Jesse. Marcus and I stay after church for a meeting and we'll come and get you later." Angel gives me a puzzled smirk but says, "okay." I point to Jared and Amy so she knows who to go to.

****

After the church service, I double check with Amy and Jared and they, of course, agree to my request. And it seems that Jesse is excited too as Angel goes to him and lets him know that she'll be joining them for lunch at the farm. Now as the auditorium is almost empty and the greetings have subsided, I notice the young man is still sitting at the other end of the front row. The hair on the back of my neck is on full alert now, because he's acting unusual and I know that we've got a security plan in place for emergencies. And, I don't usually wear my gun at church service though I have permission to do so. An advantage of being the pastor's wife. Marcus comes up and escorts the young man and me to his office which is off the auditorium. We go in and sit down, with Marcus behind the desk.

"Okay, young man. I'm Marcus." He puts his hand out to the young man to shake it, but the young man refuses the offer. He appears mad. Marcus then withdraws his hand, and we stay silent for a brief moment, then the young man says, "Why do you need your woman here? Scared?"

I can tell that Marcus is getting angry by the vein bulging on his forehead, and he tersely tells this jerk, "First of all she's my wife and will be respected as such or you can leave! Second of all, I hide nothing from her! Get on with what you have to say. I have a child waiting on us."

The young man stands up over Marcus' desk and with a mean, angry, red face tells him, "You! You are my father!"

Chapter 8
Marcus

Never in my wildest dreams would I have imagined how this weekend would unfold. Sitting at my desk with the young man looking at me like he wants to kill me, I'm stunned by the news he's delivered. To say I'm his father is not what I expected. But in studying him closely now it's obvious he's my son. He has slightly fairer skin than me, but besides that, it's like seeing a twenty-year-old version of me. When he came forward this morning I could tell he was a tortured soul, but when he said I needed to meet with him after church I knew I needed Millicent there. Now I wish she wasn't. I glance over at her and she has her hands over her face. This is not good at all.

"What's your name?" I ask. Okay. Let's start there. "Derek," is his short, snotty reply. Again, short and to the point.

After digesting this revelation, I glance back again at Millicent and she's looking back at me like I had two heads. This is my fault and after observing Derek closely I can again easily tell he's mine. It's no denying it. The next question is going to be difficult. I've been with countless women in the past. I can only eliminate my wife and... well... I wish I knew what she's thinking right now. Will she leave me? I don't know. I need to calm down. Remembering my counselor training, I take a breath. In... Out... In... Out.

"Derek. I'm sorry your angry. I need some answers and maybe you do too. Without being insensitive, whose your mother?"

Derek appears sad now. Not angry. Just sad. "My

mom's Breanna. Remember her?"

Oh yeah, I remember her alright. Funny how I was thinking about her the other day and now I see her son. Our son. "I remember your mother very well. I…"

Interrupting me, Derek loudly pounds his fist on my desk and exclaims, "You left her to raise me alone, and when we needed you she was alone. And I had no father. Don't give me your false platitudes about Jesus! I heard your sermon about serving others. Well? Where were you? TELL ME WHERE WERE YOU!" Derek sits back down and begins sobbing bitterly. Now one of the reasons I love Millicent is her compassion. My sins have come back to roost and still, she has compassion for this boy. She reaches over to him and he flinches, then she says, "Listen. I have no right in this, except that Marcus is my husband, and I know his past. Let's talk about it calmly and you can get your answers. Why don't we calmly go over to our house and talk about it? I'll get us some lunch, though it may be only a sandwich. Our daughter… I mean our child… is at a friends house and we can have some privacy, and maybe Marcus can show you some things from his college days about your mother." My Millicent is one smart cookie. She knows what I have. Again I have no secrets with her. Great idea!

But Derek will hear none of it. He gets up, towers over me like a bully and says, "Here's the deal. I don't care about you, your life, or anything else! I've been on my own for a while now and I'm in college and don't need you. But what I want is for you to suffer. This is a nice gig you have here. Want to keep it? Well, I'm not that generous. Announce your resignation by next Sunday or I'll tell everyone what you did and let's see how they'll support you then. I'll humiliate you, and what will your wifey here think about that and your daughter or whatever she is. She comes up today looking to you as her savior but you're a hypocrite and I hate you!" Just then Derek gets up and storms out of the office but not before slamming Marcus' door with the sound echoing throughout the church and pictures on the wall vibrate. The sound is deafening.

I stare at Millicent in shock. I've put my entire life and her life in jeopardy. *And what about Angel?* When Josie finds out they'll take her away because we can't support a child. Before I say anything, Millicent gets up and comes over to me. Then she leans down, kisses me, and whispers, "We'll get through this. I love you unconditionally." She gives me a half-smile. I tell her, "I'm so sorry. This is my fault and neither you nor Angel deserve this mess especially now."

"As Derek was speaking I was a little angry. Yes. I'll admit that. But what if it had been me. You know as well as I do that I was no angel, and pardon the pun, in college. I was just as bad as you, if not worse. We both prostituted ourselves. I just can't believe Breanna never told you." Yea that's a big question. And I have more. I get up and bring Millicent in for a hug. As we embrace I feel her phone vibrate. We release as she pulls her phone up and she shows me a text from Sandra.

> Sandra: M - Can we meet this afternoon? We have information. Very important!!!! and without Angel.
> Me: Okay. One hour at our house?
> Josie: One hour's okay with me.
> Sandra: Great. See you all then.

Millicent puts her phone away and tells me, "Marcus I know we've got to deal with the Derek situation but we also have Angel and that should be a focus for now. Let's go get lunch at the house, pray about these things and then we'll see." As I leave I can't but think about my hero, Dr. King. Though the situation is different he suffered, even going to jail. Going through trials helps grow us. I know that. Now it seems things are going to get worse before they get better.

****

After we get home I'm exhausted. Now Sunday afternoon is usually a busy day. I DVR a football game that I'll probably never watch. But I also try to spend time enjoying Millicent and our life. We are very busy so moments of being together are usually great and satisfying. Today is different. We ride home in silence. I can't imagine what's she's thinking now. I know what she said in my office but I have doubts about the situation. Millicent doesn't deserve this agony. And I don't know what to do about Derek. We walk in the front door of our house and Millicent goes into the kitchen to fix a couple of sandwiches. Then we sit down and eat in silence. It is very quiet. Too quiet. As we finish I offer to wash our plates and she gives me hers but she's still very quiet. *What is she thinking?*

"Marcus. While we wait for the girls let's pray about this. I feel like this is more than we can handle on our own."

We pray for guidance and discernment. For Angel. For Derek. What to do about the whole mess I've made. For forgiveness. For just about anything. As we pray I can feel my wife's agony and stress over it all. When we finish, I turn to Millie and tell her, "I feel for Derek. I was angry about my mother, and I was an angry man when I was his age. But he's put us in a difficult spot." To say the least. I sit there a moment, then Millie responds by saying, "Marcus. In all the time I've known you since you became a Christian, even when I hated you, you were an honest guy. You didn't lie or hide the truth. When the church called you ten years ago, you honestly told the congregation your story. And I've told mine in the Bible studies I've led. I think the first thing to do is tell Jill before she finds out. Then get hers and Jared's advice, not as friends, but as the Chair and Vice-Chair of the Ministry Board. Then go from there."

What Millicent says sounds reasonable. And since Jared works at the university he may know more about Derek. Derek said he went to college and besides the community college, the University of Canton would be a logical assumption as to where Derek goes to school. Thinking about it for a moment, I nervously I text Jill and Jared:

Jill and Jared: I need to talk to you ASAP. Tomorrow at 12:00 lunch in the Roman Cafe?

Jill: I can make it.

Jared: I can too. Angel having a good time.

Me: Okay. See you then. Jared - will pick up Angel about 4:30. Okay?

Jared: Sure. She likes the farm. Nick says he wants to meet you. Sarah's brother. Sorry about the other day. Amy and I are okay now.

Me: Okay and no problem bro. I'll call and set a time.

That's set for now, but *how will they react?* A knock at the door pulls me out of my thoughts and Millicent jumps up and gets the door. It's Sandra and Josie. One problem at a time.

Chapter 9
Millie

Right now, I have a headache. When we get home I go to the bathroom to take two pain relievers then come back into the living room. The events of the last couple of hours have me reeling over many things. It's overwhelming. Derek and Angel. I don't consider people to be problems, but now I'm reconsidering my position. On the one hand, Angel is a blessing, the Angel we need, so to speak. I'm scared as to how long she'll be with us. I need her here and that has been my prayer for the last couple of days. I love her like a mother, and I've never been a mother.

Derek is another matter. I know he's a part of Marcus but seeing how he's blackmailing my husband makes me furious inside. I know all about Breanna. I was there. She strung Marcus along like a sick puppy and mysteriously left college. I know Marcus regretted what happened, but Breanna left on her own and Derek may have some answers, but we're not gonna get them while he is trying to get his revenge. He views Marcus as some sort of crook disguised as a pastor. It's too bad that too many pastors and TV evangelists have been like that, but I know my husband. He's not perfect, and he's not broken his vows to me. He's honest and caring. I remember him even after we started dating how he wanted to make amends, but could never locate Breanna. The guilt was something that hurt us in our dating life. He went to counseling for a while to deal with guilt and with his injury in college. But when we talked about it and as time went on, the guilt subsided, but I can now tell its back and I hate it. I was right in saying that Marcus and I are cut from the same cloth with our pasts, but

Breanna had a child by him, and I never will. That makes me more motivated to keep Angel. Because I feel like she's mine. Maybe that's too possessive, but that's how I feel.

When the knock from the door echos in the room I go get it. I open the door to see Sandra and Josie. Sandra. What can I say? She's dating Micah, and I hope she sees what she will be getting into with that man. He's got issues.

And Josie. Well, I know more about her. At eighteen she was going to get married to Myron, who was twenty-one and a soldier in Iraq. Her family is wealthy and discouraged the marriage, not only because Myron was from the 'wrong side of the tracks' but he was also a soldier. So much so that she distanced herself from them. When he was killed in the line of duty, Josie changed. She never dates and seems to have never recovered from her grief. Every time I'm around her a cloud of sadness hangs over her head. Especially around babies. She volunteers in the nursery and when I see her rocking some of the babies, she seems so very sad. But despite all that, she's good at her job. Maybe too good.

"Sandra. Josie. Come on in. Want coffee?" I'm nothing if not polite.

"No thanks we can't stay long. I need to go see Micah," Sandra says. They both sit down in the living room and Marcus says his greetings and we sit next to each other. I go and hold his hand.

Sandra seems to be taking the lead so she pulls out a file folder with papers in it and opens it, then she begins. "Millie. Marcus. First of all, you have been very helpful in finding information about Angel. Let's start with some information and Josie is gonna give you a copy of some of it. Enough to enroll her in school. Angel, as she's called, is actually… **Frances Angel Peters**. Angel is fourteen as you deduced Millie, is in the ninth grade at Neemon High School in Akron.   Her mother… Dee. Dee was a… prostitute in Akron. Also used drugs. She was found in their apartment January 2nd by the Akron PD who were called by another tenant. Millie? She was murdered. Two shots. The Akron PD thinks that Big Daddy was her pimp and that he may have been trying to get Angel involved in the business. Big Daddy is a lower level drug supplier but his big business is prostitution and maybe human trafficking. Big Daddy is an alias for George Kelly, a creep and lowlife who has a record a mile long. A BOLO, or 'Be on the Lookout' alert, went out for Big Daddy the next day but he hasn't been seen. According to the school, Angel is an excellent student but they've never seen her mother, not even her teachers in elementary school saw her. She has no after-school activities, and it appears that Angel took care of her mother and was raising herself. And, probably doing a good job of it."

Sandra stops then pulls out the picture of George Kelly. What a creep. Sandra then says, "About Angel. We think she saw her mother killed or is a witness to something. I don't think Big Daddy will come after her, because he doesn't know where she is. Let's keep it that way though. For now."

Just great. We have Derek and that problem. Angel is now a known quantity but now we have to deal with the mysterious Big Daddy. Time to keep my handgun on me. I have a concealed carry permit and have a small revolver that is on a waist holster.

Josie chimes in and carefully informs us both, "I have her school records here and I hope you can get her in school ASAP. I'll need to go to court this week and get the temporary order put in place for a longer term, but the judge will ask about school." She hands me a thick file.

Marcus stares back at me as if he wants approval, then asks, "Will Canton Academy be okay?" Everyone agrees. That is where Jesse goes so Angel will have a friend there and it is a great Christian school in the city. So we agreed that either Marcus or I will go tomorrow to get her in school, but tonight we have to deal with a grieving child and to assure her of her safety. My headache just got worse.

"Did Angel's mother have any family?" I ask.

"According to what we have no known family exists but we still don't know who Angel's father is. It could have been a customer. If so, we may never know. She's fourteen. A DNA test may help but that'll take weeks." Sandra says that then glances down at her watch.

Josie then leans over and takes my hand. "Millie, it's going to be okay. We'll go so you can tell Angel." So we all get up and they both get ready to leave. As they head to the door, I tell Josie, "Marcus and I haven't talked about it yet, but if it's possible, we would like..." I stop then turn to Marcus who gives me an approving smile. "We would like to keep Angel with the possibility of adopting her later, if that's possible and if she's willing."

"Of course. I'll do everything in my power to make that happen. But no promises yet. Be patient. I wish more of my clients had a safe place like this to go to." Josie leaves that comment hanging as she and Sandra leave. My headache has gotten worse.

Chapter 10
Marcus

After leaving Millicent at the house I am on my way
to pick up from Jared our Angel. We now know who she is
and what she's been through. I want to hear sometime how
she got from Akron to Canton, which is thirty miles away.
Yet, I feel like she is our miracle. And we certainly need
one since Derek showed up. I think I've said it before but
Millicent and I should have stayed in the Caribbean. But
then we wouldn't have met Angel. I'm making my way to
Amish country in Wayne County, which is just southwest of
us about twenty minutes away. Jared and Amy's farm is
near the county border. As I leave the city, the hills and
trees are glistening with snow and today is a sunny day.
For northeast Ohio it's warm. About 25 degrees. But the
sun feels good. I am driving towards their house thinking
about the day. Angel is certainly on my mind, but Derek is a
puzzle that needs to be solved. I'm being blackmailed, or
am I? I just don't know what to do. So when I'm stumped I
go to the One who knows all things.

*Oh, Father. I've confessed my sins in the past and
I know you have forgiven them. But that doesn't mean that
there are no consequences. So I'm in a tough spot now. I
give it all to you. Angel. Derek. My ministry. And of
course, Millicent. Help our marriage endure and provide us
our needs. Let it be your will. Give me guidance on the
course ahead. In your Son Jesus' name. Amen.*

After my prayer, I get a refreshing sense of peace in
my heart. I turn on to the farm road and quickly count all of
the cars in the driveway. It seems Jared has his whole
family out here. I park and get out, taking in the warmth of

the sun. This is the first sunny day in a week. I wished I'd been able to take advantage of it. I go up the stairs towards the front door and knock. After a couple of seconds, Jared opens his door.

"Marcus! How's it going brother," Jared says as he brings me in for a brotherly hug. Jared is older than me and was a young professor twenty years ago when I was in college. He also had a counseling practice as a licensed psychologist and counseled me after my injury senior year. From then on after my sessions ended, we became friends. Jared is a pillar in the church and his life with Sarah, and now Amy, is the life of a novel or sappy movie. After we release our hug Jared points to the kitchen where Sofia, Amy, Charlotte, Mavis, and Robin are there, with Ellis in a high chair. Food is spread out on the counter and the smell permeates the room. My stomach growls. Sofia is giving a cooking lesson. "Sorry, you and Millie couldn't make it today. Did your meeting go well? That guy looked rather upset." Understatement of the decade. I'm awakened from my food coma with Jared's comment, so I reply, "That's why I need to talk to you and Jill tomorrow. I have a major problem." Jared glances at me, but before he says anything Amy yelps from the kitchen, "Hey Marcus. Jesse and Angel went out toward the pond for a walk. She was so helpful today at lunch. We have so much food do you want some for dinner for you and Millie? Angel's probably not hungry but I'll fix leftovers for her too."

"Uh huh" is all I could get out. I need to get an anti-dating daddy t-shirt. I'm not pleased about Jesse's closeness with Angel, but Millicent and I need to get on the same page first before we talk to Angel about it. But there are other pressing matters. Amy gives me a strange and curious smirk then goes back into the kitchen. Jared, seeing my worried face, touches me on the arm and tells me, "Marcus. I'm your friend and brother in Christ. Let's go into the den and talk. No one will interrupt us there." So I follow him.

When we sit down in his den, I notice there's some work that still needs to be down in here but it's nice. "So, Marcus. What's going on? Is it Angel? A meeting tomorrow has me concerned and I just want to help you."

After staring down at the floor for a moment, I move my eyes back up to Jared. He's been my friend for a long time, longer than Millicent. I want to tell him about Angel and Derek, and well, just pour my heart out. As I move to the den my tears flow from my eyes. And I'm not a crier. It's been too much. After I finish I slowly glance back at Jared and he seems to be ready to listen what I have to say.

****

"Tell me what's going on my friend. I've known you a long time Marcus and I can tell that these last few days have taken a toll on you," Jared tells me as we sit down next to the fireplace, one of two in the house. As I peer at the mesmerizing fire that blazes below the mantel, I can't help but wonder about the path I chose. *Will my ministry end just like that? What about Millicent and Angel?* So I turn. *Too many questions and not enough answers.* I turn to Jared who's sitting beside me and begin.

"Jared. Besides Angel, we have a problem that can impact my entire ministry. You remember how I was when I was as a student at U of Canton, right?" Jared nods and I can see he is here to listen.

"That young man this morning, was...is... my son. Over twenty years ago I had an intimate relationship with Breanna Stoltz, a former student. It lasted about three months. The relationship ended when she left me a note saying that she wanted to break up and to never see her again. I was devastated. For several years I wrote letters and tried to make contact but gave up before I got married. Millicent knew about our relationship and all of my deficiencies when I was young, dumb, and stupid. But I never knew about her... our son. I never knew until today. And now he is blackmailing me into quitting the church as some sort of revenge for my abandoning him. I'm at a loss as to what to do." I sit there and return my gaze to the hypnotic fire.

"Marcus," Jared starts. "I'm sorry you have to go through this. I remember Breanna. She was a student of mine in my Psychology 101 class. She hardly showed up for class and after some efforts on my part, she showed up a little. She always was kind of hungover and well... she ended up failing, but you didn't hear that from me. I saw her a couple of times around campus. Our school was and isn't that big. So Derek thinks that the congregation will throw you out over something that happened before you were redeemed. Um mm."

I can see the wheels turning in Jared's head. "Friend. Let me talk with Jill tonight and let's talk some more tomorrow when we get together. All is not lost yet. So let me pray for you here." And so he did. As we finish, I hear the front door open and Angel's laughter is heard throughout the house. Jesse's as well. We get up and go back to the great room where I see Jesse holding Angel's hand. *Uh huh.* Definitely need my t-shirt. We definitely need to have a discussion with her and Robin. But now's not the time. I paste on a smile and view the happy couple. "Hey, Jesse? Thanks again for the booth today. Great job keeping up." I give him a fist bump. Well, my bump may have been a little hard as Jesse shakes his hand a bit. Oh well. I go to the kitchen and see not only the women, but Nathan, Kyle, and a person I do not know in there, with an arm in a sling. Greg must be out of town. Jared comes up and introduces me to Nick, Sarah's brother. Sarah was Jared's first wife before she was killed several years ago. "Nick, you are welcome anytime at church," I say. Then I add, "I appreciate your service. What did you do?"

"I was a chaplain before I got shot. I was in an army hospital for a while, then I will take a discharge after my leave expires. I decided to come here for a bit when Jared offered the bunkhouse. I'm not really sure of my next move yet. I might look for a church to pastor, but... we'll see.," Nick told me as everyone carefully listened. I peek over at Amy who seems to be smiling. I file this information for later. Too much on my mind for now. So I reply, "Well, let me know if I can help." I get a good feeling about Nick.

He gives me an obligatory "okay". *But of course, how can I promise that when I could be out of the ministry by next week?*

So I turn back to Angel whose let go of Jesse's hand and tell her, "Angel sweetheart. Ready to go. It's almost dark and we need to get back. Can you text Millicent to let her know we're on our way and we're bringing dinner?' "Yes sir" was her reply and I hand her my phone as we haven't given her one yet. I feel old when she says that, like I don't deserve it. I go over in the kitchen to pick up my food and thank all of the ladies for their hospitality as Angel and I head for the door then the car.

****

As we head back to our house with the smell of delicious food in the rear of the car, the silence is almost deafening. So I decide to break the ice. "Angel. We talked to Josie today." That got her ears perking up as she gets a curious look on her face. "Millicent and I will cover the entire conversation at home with you because we want no secrets from you about what this situation is all about. But we did ask about keeping you for the long term. How do you feel about that?"

Now Angel seems surprised and smiles at that. She immediately asks, "How long is a long time." Good question. Now for my carefully worded answer. "Well. We hope to keep you for… forever, but that is not up to us. It's up to the courts and you have a say in that. But we need to work on getting you in school and showing that we can be a family. And that starts with honesty. Do you understand?"

Angel stares down at the floor and mumbles, "I don't want anything to happen to you or Millie. I love you both." Now I know at least some of the reason she's been holding back. She's trying to protect us. While admirable, she needs to understand we need to protect her. She's never known a stable family in the sense of having a home with some semblance of normalcy in it. For most of her life, she's cared for others and not herself. She's a shining example, albeit misguided, of my sermon this morning.

"It won't honey and we love you too. Don't forget that." I reach for her hand as we drive back home.

****

     I pull in our driveway, noticing that the streetlight is on. It gets dark really early in northeast Ohio and at 6:00 it can be unsafe out at night. Our neighborhood is not in the best of places, but we take care of each other as best as we can. Millicent and I know all of our neighbors and with Mavis now on our side, that helps. When we get up to the house and open the front door, Millicent greets us with a smile and we go in with the food. Sofia outdoes herself today. Yummy! When we finish, Angel does the dishes, and both Millicent and I go into the living room. We're sitting in there when Angel comes in and says, "All finished." Then she sits across from us. Millicent leans over to me and whispers to me, "Marcus. It's time. Let me do the talking for now." For that, I completely agree.

Chapter 11
Millie

While Marcus was gone to pick up Angel, I spent time in prayer. For Marcus. For me. For Angel, and for Derek. Even though he's acting like a jerk, I still feel compelled. In my mind as far as Derek is concerned I feel like Marcus and I should fight this but how? I go into the kitchen after praying in the living room and reading my Bible to make some coffee. My phone pinged a few minutes ago that Angel and Marcus will be bringing food home and that they're leaving Jared and Amy's now. I need to thank them when all of this is over. And I hope Sofia cooked. As I hear the front door open I see Marcus and Angel come in and take off their jackets. Then they bring the bags of food in and I get some plates out as the coffee maker begins to percolate. We silently get plates and fix our food. Shrimp Fajitas with onions and peppers. Hmm. Humph. Great! We bow for prayer then eat in silence again. I wonder what Marcus and Angel talked about in the car? Regardless, we finish eating and Sofia volunteers to do the dishes and I agree. Then I fix Marcus and me our cups of coffee and we go into the living room to sit. Just before Angel comes in I lean over to Marcus and tell him, "Marcus. It's time. Let me do the talking for now." He nods in agreement. Just then Angel indicates she's finished the dishes and sits across from us waiting for the hammer to fall. I can tell she knows something is up. So I start.

"Angel. First of all, we care a lot about you. And I don't know what you know so far, but Detective Coblentz and Miss Bailey came by today to update us on the case. We did tell them that we wish for you to remain here long-term and possibly adopt you. It's been three days Angel and I know its hard, but…" I stop to let that sink in. Three days. "Angel we know most everything about you. You're *Frances Angel Peters* aren't you?"

"Yes ma'am. I'm sorry I kept things from you." Angel begins to sob and grabs a tissue from the coffee table. Then she wipes her eyes and continues. "My mother was killed." Then she breaks down and I go over to her to give her a hug while Marcus stays on the couch.

"Sweetie. We know and we're very sorry for your loss. It must've been hard to lose your mother like that. But things have changed a bit for us and we have to do things the right way. As a new believer, you'll learn that we have a certain life to live, not because of the rules, but because as we get closer to God, we want to do His will. And one thing is honesty. Do you understand what I'm saying?"

I stop to make sure Angel is aware of the need to be open with us. This will build trust and a foundation for the future. Our future. By the way, that reminds me. It may be difficult but we also need to talk to her about Derek. If we want her to be honest then we have to as well. I'm just not sure what to say to that. I make a mental note to talk to Marcus about that later tonight.

"Angel, we know everything about you and Big Daddy. We also know that you are safe here and the police are on the lookout for him for your mother's murder. Did he kill your mother?"

Angel wiped her tears again, stares at the floor and shakes her head 'yes'. Then she added, "He's my father. And, he wanted me in the business." Well… we didn't know everything.

Marcus gets up from the couch and goes into our bedroom to what I assume is to make a call to Sandra or Josie. The revelation that Big Daddy is Angel's father just changed the game and made it even more dangerous. "Angel. He may be your biological father, but he's no daddy. Well, that may be his name but he does not act like one. *A true father protects his children, not sell their bodies into prostitution and human trafficking!*" I cannot believe that monster wants Angel for her body's worth! What a creep!   I hug her and we both start shedding tears.

After a short time, I hear the door close to our bedroom and Marcus comes out with his cell phone on his ear. "Okay Sandra we'll be looking for them and we'll take precautions." He hangs up and sits back down. The lights are on inside and it's dark outside but fortunately, a lamppost is right outside lighting up the sidewalk. If anyone came up, we would know. Marcus and I gaze at each other trying to figure out our next steps. Then Angel says gets up and barely gets out, "Marcus. Millie... I care about you. Big Daddy will want me back. But Mom was trying to protect me from that life she led. And I took care of her because she was on drugs most of the time. She didn't want that life for me and kept me out of the apartment..." A door knock interrupts as Marcus gets up to answer the door as if he knows who it is. He opens and Sandra comes in. "Sandra," I say noting that Angel is not happy she's here.

The detective turns towards Angel and after nodding her head at Marcus and me, tells her in no uncertain terms, "Angel. We need to talk."

****

A couple of minutes later, we have moved to the kitchen island and Sandra has pulled out her phone and placed it in recording mode. I offer coffee and she declines. Then Sandra faces Angel and states emphatically, "Angel? I need to know everything about your mother's murder. We need a record of it so I'm going to use my phone to dictate what you say. So start at the beginning. Marcus. Millie? No interruptions. Got it?" Now I feel like I'm in trouble. But we indicate that we will comply.

"I was coming home from school. The bus lets us off at the end of the street so I had to walk a few blocks. That day, I saw Big Daddy's new *Texliy* black sports car."

Marcus lets out a whistle. "Texliy? Wow. Pimping must be lucrative. That's a $250,000 vehicle!" I elbow Marcus and go "Shush!" Angel giggles, then continues. "Yea that car is not bad. Anyway. I go by that car and up the stairs. The door was cracked open and I look inside to see Mom lying on the floor…" Angel chokes up and starts crying again. Then she blurts out, "there's a pool of blood." She is tortured by the image of her mother lying on the floor with blood. My heart breaks for this child to have seen such a heinous crime. Angel wipes her eyes with her sleeve and starts again. "I tried to wake her but then I saw Big Daddy come out of my room. He said he's glad to see me and he had a gun in his hand. That's when I ran for the door and I heard him chasing me but I got away. I hitched a couple of rides and walked some until I got to the house where you found me Millie."

We sit there a moment to let all of the new information sink in, then Sandra asks Angel, "How do you know Big Daddy is your father, Angel?" Umm. Interesting question. Angel peeks back up with those swollen eyes.

Those eyes. They're tired, and evidence of crying and sadness are evident. It's been a very long day and I'm tired too. As I look up at Marcus I see the struggle that he's going through as well.

"My mother told me last year," Angel replies to Sandra. Sandra then turns off the phone recorder and gets up. Then she tells all of us, "I'm going to assign a police officer to patrol the area, just as a precaution. I still think you're not in danger, but to be safe, let's take some extra precautions. Is Angel going to school tomorrow?"

I reply, "Yes we're going to try to get her in now that I have her school records." Then I survey Angel and in a reassuring voice tell her that it's going to be okay. She smiles, then gazes at Marcus who gives her an approving nod. Okay for now.

****

After Sandra leaves, we decide to relax a bit. Frankly, we're too tired to take in more after this day. And, I still need to talk privately with Marcus about the Derek situation. As she sits in the living room I notice Angel yawning and nodding off a bit and it's only 8:30. Maybe she needs to just go to bed. A teenager needs rest, right? Well, I'm forty this year and I need mine. So I tell Angel, "Honey, go get ready to bed and I'll be up in a little while." As if a zombie, Angel goes on upstairs to get ready. And after a couple of days, she's gotten into a routine for bed and with her new stuff, I'm glad. Angel is a very compliant child. Or young woman. I have to keep reminding myself of that.

I head to the master bedroom and Marcus follows me after finishing up in the study. Sunday nights are a time where he gets his calendar ready for the week and he tries to get his evening prayers in. I'm sure he's been distracted and I wish I could relieve him of his pain, but tonight's not the night. As he enters the room I can tell he's burdened by the day. But he starts with some interesting news.

"Angel and Jesse are getting a little close. They were holding hands when I was there, and I'm concerned. I didn't think it is right to confront Angel until we talk. I think we need to sit down with her and give her some guidance and rules on dating. I guess we need to decide on those rules."

This day just gets better and better. I'm absorbing what Marcus said for a moment. Then I come up to him and give him a hug, a very friendly hug. Then I kiss him. Hard. Maybe tonight will be a good stress reliever. We release, then I tell him, "Everyone's going to be okay Marcus."

"That's what Jared said earlier," he told me with a slightly sexy smirk on his face. "So what did he say? You must've told him about Derek?"

"He's gonna talk to Jill tonight and we'll talk at lunch more tomorrow so tonight we can't borrow trouble, I guess." Easier said than done. "I love you Millicent and I always will no matter what happens."

When he calls me 'Millicent' it sends chills down my spine. *My stars!* As I start to kiss him again a knock comes from our door. We break free and I go to the door to see Angel. She says, "Uh... Millie? I need your help. I've..." She leans over to whisper to me "I've started." Well, that'll put a damper on things. So, I glance back at Marcus then say, "Angel needs me so I'll be back after I get her... ready for bed." It's been a long day.

Chapter 12
Marcus
Around Martin Luther King Holiday

Today is a national holiday and the church offices are closed. There are also no classes at the University of Canton, but the businesses on campus are open like the cafes because students are on campus for classes to start tomorrow. So Millicent and I have the day off. But, unfortunately, some schools are in session. I'm not sure why but that needs to change. Before I haven't had a need to care about Canton Academy, but now as a father, be it temporary or hopefully permanent, we as parents now need to step up. Like every day, I get up early the in morning to have prayer and devotional time. It is an opportunity to commune with God on a personal level. *I need to talk to Angel about this.* So I make a note to do that this evening. Also, we need to talk to her about Derek.

Later in the morning after devotions and breakfast on most days, Millicent and I drive separately to the gym for a morning workout. She normally has an early self-defense class she teaches on Mondays. Then we get to church by 9 am for a staff meeting. We have had an assistant pastor vacancy for over a year now, but we have had several interns from the college and directors. I am fortunate to have a highly capable executive assistant, Deidra Holmes, who has been divorced for a couple of years after her husband left her for another woman. Deidra has a five-year-old son who's just started school this year. Her husband was a jerk of the highest order. Pastor's aren't supposed to call people names but the thought is there just the same.

Angel is a welcome disruption to our house, and Millicent and I have to adjust to the new paradigm that is all things Angel. Today things will be different. Millicent is going to register Angel for classes, and when we told her last night about the school and that Jesse attends there. I'm not sure whether she's more excited about the school or seeing Jesse as they're both in the ninth grade. They'll probably have classes together. So we have to monitor that. And, today is my upcoming meeting with Jared and Jill, which will be anxious.

I make my way to the gym after kissing my wife goodbye and giving well wishes to Angel. At the gym, I'm having a hard time concentrating on my reps. I like to go through the stations and do 3 sets of 10. But with missing some last week and today's lack of focus I'm off. "Yo Marcus," my close friend and Jill's husband says. "Hey there, Cole. See you made it out of the bed this morning," I give it back to Cole. "How are the wonder twins?" I ask.

"Great. Both got early acceptance to the University this fall." Allison and Walt are seniors at Canton Academy.

"By the way. Did Jill tell you about Angel?"

"Yea, I saw her yesterday. Beautiful child. Hope she'll work out with you. Planning to keep her long-term?" Cole asks.

"That's the plan, but God will have to work out the details my friend."

I continue my reps and Cole is now on the machine next to me. He's leaner than me and not in the best of shape. Jill and Cole have had a couple of marital issues in the past, but seem to be on the right path. Having an autistic genius is hard for them, but Allison is a gift from God and Walt is as well. He protects her as a decent brother should. As I finish the last weightlifting machine, Cole finishes as well and we head to the locker room. It's empty. So Cole takes advantage of the situation so he touches my arm to get my attention and leans over so no one else can hear, though no one is in here this early.

"Marcus. Jared and Jill were on the phone last night and they talked about your situation. You know this guy could be arrested for blackmail."

"No, I don't want that. He's my… son, and despite that, if I do that everyone will find out anyway."

"Yea well it's an option. But Jill and I 100% support you and Millicent. And, I bet 90% of the church will too." Cole let that comment fill the air as others came in the locker room. I mouth 'thank you" to my friend.   As we leave we say our goodbyes and head out.

****

The morning goes by very slowly as I await the meeting at high noon. I go by the empty church office to open my mail that is mostly junk. Then I sit at my desk, reply to some emails, and surf the internet for any intel about Breanna. Nothing. Derek has some junior college pictures from Florida, and some statistics on football, but nothing of note. No social media. Nothing. When it gets closer to noon, I lock up and head over to campus to talk to Jared and Jill. As I head over my thoughts go back to Breanna and the last time I saw her.

She was a little distant, but nothing unusual. To be honest, we partied so hard the night before, my hangover was in full swing that morning. She didn't drink or smoke a joint though, which was odd for her. Breanna stayed with me that night and then when I got back home, she was gone, leaving only a note. I couldn't believe it. I was devastated and tried to find her, but she had packed up her dorm room and left without a word to her roommate. I found out later she had withdrawn that day too. This was planned, pure and simple. I even went to her home in Pennsylvania, and she wasn't there either. Her mom said she left, but was either unwilling or unable to give me information. She didn't have a cell phone. Heck. That was a long time ago. Twenty years, or was it twenty-one?

I arrive on campus and park near the Roman Cafe and enter. Sure enough, Jared and Jill are sitting there in the corner away from people. Fortunately being a holiday it's not crowded, and I don't see Derek either. Good sign. I go over and shake Jared's hand and Jill's too. These have been my friends for many years.

Once we get our order we sit. I'm not hungry and order coffee. It's my fifth cup today. I start. "First I want to apologize to you for putting the church in a bad position to deal with this. If you feel I should quit tell me now." I stop hoping that's not the case, but I need to gauge where they are on the issue.

"Marcus?" Jill responds to me as she eases into the conversation. "Don't be silly. But, I'll be honest. This is not gonna be easy, and I don't know the outcome, but this could be an opportunity. We've grown so fast and now look at the church. We have so many ministries going on that we need to add staff. What church can say that around here? Most churches are shrinking but we've engaged millennials, boomers, and well... The vision of a cross-generational, multiracial church is being realized because of your leadership and God's guidance. Maybe this is a sign that we need to see who will stay and who will go. I know most of the people that go to the church and my bet is that it'll work itself out."

Jared has been mostly silent and eating his chicken sandwich. I quietly survey him hoping for any words of wisdom, but he's mostly silent. Strange. Jill goes on. "Boys? It's time to put your big pants on now. I don't like blackmail. I think we should just tell the church and let the chips fall where they may. Honesty is always best."

"How do you propose we do that?" I ask.

Jared finally lights up and tells us both, "I have a thought. When we had some issues a few years ago and a few faculty members were upset about not getting a raise, Dr. Porter put them on the spot by embarrassing them. He laid out the budget, the issues, everything. Then he said this. 'If you feel that someone else can do better then, I'll leave if the majority of you think so. Then he called for a no-confidence vote. He won of course. Can't we do that Jill?"

"It's doable, but the ministry board will have to approve and then we have to notify the church of a business meeting for Sunday after the last service. I don't like it though. Putting Marcus' fate in the hands of people like that Davis family and others can be dangerous. But … Oh. Marcus what are your thoughts?"

I sit there thinking about the circumstances. I would have to come clean with everything. But I've done that before. I was honest when I can to the church. On the other hand, I also don't want to split the church down the middle. So I say a quick prayer in my heart about this and an idea bubbles in my head. Without thinking I replay, "I'll agree, but only if I get to state my case Sunday, and I want… 70%

vote of confidence, not 51%. I need the vast majority of the members to support us or it won't work. I'm laying that out as my fleece." I stop to see the shock on Jared and Jill's face.

Jill tentatively continues. "Well… okay… But we need to have a board meeting tonight. Are you available Jared? Marcus? I think it would be best if you don't show up. It may be easier and it will also protect you should it go down badly." I agree and Jill texts everyone about the meeting tonight at the church. I guess I'll have to go over this episode again. As we finish Jill tells me "I hope you know what you're doing." Me too.

Chapter 13
Millie

"Millie, do you think I'll fit in at school?" Angel asks me in the car on the way to register her. I glance over to her keeping my eyes on the road. "Well. I'm not sure, to be honest. You know Jesse so that's a positive, but some kids are hard on the newbie. There will be an adjustment. Going to a private school will also be different for you. The Academy is a Christian school so that may help you as you learn more about your newfound faith. But you can always tell us anything. We may not always be happy, but we want you to feel safe with us." I'm trying to continue to reinforce that we're okay. Angel seems to accept my answer. We pull up to the school and park in the visitor's lot. We are buzzed in the front door and go to the office where we find the school secretary. Hazel Zimmer has been here for a few years since Jenny Akers retired. "Mornin' Hazel," I great her with a smile. "This is Angel and we're here to see Principal Roberts. Is she in? She's expecting us." I texted her yesterday. I put my arm around Angel because she seems a little nervous.

"Oh yeah. She told me. She's available. Let me get her on my phone and see if she's ready for you."

After waiting a couple of minutes Hazel escorts us to the office. When we go we are greeted by an eager Margaret Roberts, another acquaintance of mine who goes to church across town. She's been principal for about ten years. She just looks marvelous, having lost 100 pounds over that last couple of years. An inspiration to us all. Margaret says, "Millie? Great to see you again and this must be Angel. Uhh... Frances Angel Peters." They shake hands and Angel is very quiet. Probably nerves. Using her full name didn't help.

"Margaret I have her records here and a copy of the court order giving us custody. Is there anything else we need in order to get Angel in school?"

Margaret takes the file and peers over it for a moment. She finally finishes, and tells us both, "Nope. Everything's in order. I can assign a fellow ninth grader to be her escort for the day, but we should probably start her tomorrow because the guidance office will need to get a schedule, a locker, and other things. Just come in tomorrow and see Hazel. I also have some forms for you to fill out, Millie. Emergency contacts, confidentiality forms and the like. Stuff we have to do nowadays. You can take them home and Angel can bring them tomorrow. Sound okay?"

We both nod our heads. Oh well. Tomorrow it is. Then Margaret asks Angel, "so you know anybody here that could help you by being your guide the first day?"

Angel over-eagerly replies, "Oh yes, Jesse is here and he already told me he would be willing to guide me!" Oh brother.

"Okay, then, I guess. Jesse's still kind of new too, but that should be okay. I'll arrange it tomorrow."

We get up to shake hands, and leave with the hope that school goes okay. But I need to talk to Angel about the facts of life. We head out and I tell Angel we need to stop by the mansion to meet with Amy about the plans. On our way, we ride in silence. Then as we pull up to the mansion I see the Moore SUV. As we get out and head inside I hear giggles and laughs. I call out "hello" and suddenly some crashing noises occur. We go in and find Jared and Amy in… well… I'm not quite sure what we interrupted, but it appears to be a make out session. Jared is holding Amy next to a table and well… I clear my throat, and Amy stares at me, then Angel, and says, "Hi Millie." Then she giggles again. Maybe I need to give Amy the facts of life talk too.

"Uh...Hi," I reply. So awkward here. I glance at Angel who's holding back a laugh. She's smiling and that's progress.

"I'll pick you up when you're ready. Remember I have a noon meeting," Jared whispers to Amy as he makes his way out.

"Sorry about that," Amy says as we go into the study where the plans are. As I go to the makeshift table I can't help but notice Angel wandering around. As I think about her, something comes to me. *Maybe it would be good for Angel to be involved in the Sarah Moore House?* This could be a community service project that will get Angel involved in something that could take her mind off of the tragedy in her life. I know she can get high school credits so maybe it would be good for her to keep her mind off of losing her mother and the Big Daddy saga. So I go for it. "Angel, I'd like you to be involved in this project too. To not only help us but to give me insight into some things I may have a hard time with. Do you want to be involved?"

Angel smiles. With a happy expression of relief and joy she says, "Absolutely. I'd love to see what this is all about?" We spend the next hour going over the plans and Angel does offer some thoughts. Some good, some not. But she's involved. That's what matters. As I glance down at my watch, it's about 11:30 and just then Jared comes in and announces, "Ready to leave sweetheart?" We all say our goodbyes, as the weight of Marcus' meeting at noon suddenly is on my heart. I say a silent prayer. Then I feel like I need to do something with Angel, so I ask her to eat out for lunch. Of course, she says 'yes' because she knows I can't cook, unless she wants a grilled cheese and tomato soup again.

****

A few minutes later we arrive at *Nacho Taco*, the Mexican restaurant that's never crowded but is good and cheap. The have 99-cent loaded tacos that are to die for. We sit in the back to have privacy, then give our orders and I begin to talk as we eat chips and salsa. Not bad food. After saying grace, I observe Angel who's sitting across from me. So I begin.

"Angel? How do you like living with us so far?"

"I love it. I just wish I knew if it will be long-term or not." Yea me too.

"I know. It's tough but we'll pray about it and see what happens."

"Millie?" Angel begins as she's staring down at the table. A tell of hers is she looks away or down when she asks a question but is afraid of the answer. "Why did God let my mom die?"

"Well..." I begin. "We all struggle with the question, 'why does God let bad things happen, even to good people?' Today is a cold day and that window over there is fogged up, right?" I point to the big window near us and she acknowledges it. "Well, sometimes we can't understand God's intentions on why he intervenes in some ways and not others. What's His purpose in things? Why is life hard sometimes? That window is frosted over. Fogged up. We can't see outside with our limited vision, but God can. He has the ability to see the past, present, and future at the same time. We can only see the present. So we have to trust that God knows what he's doing because we're partially blind and he's not. I guess that's the best way to describe it. One other way of looking at it is that tough times can be opportunities for growth. We exercise our bodies to build muscle and sometimes we have muscle aches and pains, but we should do it anyway to keep our bodies fit. I believe that God uses tough times to mold our character and develop us. If everything was peaches and cream all the time, we wouldn't grow. Instead, we'd get lazy and whither like a plant."

I pick up a chip and eat it with the salsa of course and Angel does the same. She seems satisfied with my answer for now. It's probably not the best one, but it the only one I've got. A minute later our food comes. We eat in silence and finish up but I don't want to go yet. I want to have a woman to woman talk. By the way, another thing I notice about Angel is that she doesn't like to eat a meal and talk. Silence is her thing there. Also, I'm glad she's getting an appetite. She's still taking medicine, and she appears 100% better than the other day, which seems like a lifetime ago.

"Angel. Listen. Can I give you some advice about boys? Marcus and I have noticed your affection for Jesse." Angel eyes me as if I stepped on a landmine. Okay. Not the best topic. "Well...okay." Angel stares at me with a shy, reddened face as if she wants to say, 'I don't really want to talk about this.' Tough. She's getting it anyway.

"I learned some hard lessons in my life and you've seen more in life than anyone should see. First, you can come to me for anything. Anything that you need help with. I want us to have a great relationship regardless of what happens. You are very special to me. Don't ever forget that. One of the things that pleases Jesus is that we keep our bodies pure before marriage. I know that is different than what society says, but I've found in counseling young girls that it's the best course. And to wait until marriage is a gift to the husband but also to Jesus...."

Angel interrupts. "Oh... that's it? Don't worry about that. I don't want to have sex until I find the right guy and get married. If a boy doesn't like that then he can just go on because I've got no time for games. Jesse and I are... friends, but... we're taking it slow. I'm new and I need a friend. Jesse is a gentleman. And a strong believer." Smart girl. Very smart girl. I'm surprised by her answer.

In relief I reply to my darling Angel, "I hope it stays that way, but remember. Protect yourself by not putting yourself in a difficult position by being alone with a boy in a bedroom or something. And, Angel? I may sound like a prude, but I say this in love. I..."

I stop and begin to reconsider what I will say next, but I want to be honest with her about me. So I go on. "I was very promiscuous in high school and it lead to some bad behaviors later. And I still struggle with guilt. Let God be your guide. Study the Word and feel free to ask Marcus or me any questions. Not just about this but about everything. Do you understand?"

"Yes, ma'am," Angel politely replied. I hope that is enough for now. But more in-depth talks are for later.

Then she moves onto another subject. "Millie? Why do you carry a gun on your backside? I mean... guns make me nervous especially after..."

"Oh, sweetheart? For one thing, I have a concealed carry permit. That means the government gives me permission to carry my weapon. And it is unusual for a pastor's wife to carry I know. I guess I want to feel safe. I do, but well...?" Oh, the words to say to a young lady. "Well. I guess the best way to explain it is that I don't want the world to win. I want to be able to protect myself in case Marcus is not around. No one else will. God protects us, yes, but we have to be willing to take action ourselves. And, I'm careful and obey the law. I didn't bring my weapon in the restaurant because they have a sign, though I'm sure a sign will never stop someone if he or she wanted to do harm." Then I observe Angel. Not a political discussion for today. "Angel I also studied karate in college and teach classes on self-defense on Tuesday nights. They're called the Mama Bear Self-Defense Club, and I guess the best explanation is that if I go down I'm going down swinging. While God intended us to not seek vengeance I do believe he intends for us to protect ourselves from criminals and the like." I hope I explained it well so I take a swig of my water and hope she accepts my answer at face value. Instead, I got a surprise.

"My mother couldn't defend herself. But I want to. Do you think I could learn? Self-defense that is." Poor Angel.

"Of course. You can attend the class if you like but you'll be the youngest in there. And we'll do it together." I move on to my next topic.

"On the subject of togetherness, of this we want you to know that as long as you're a part of this family, and we hope that is... a long time. A very long time. We need to talk about Marcus. He's going through a difficult period now, and well… you're going to hear some talk around church about it. You see, as a pastor, some people think Marcus has to be perfect. He also had a past life before he came to Christ and while he is forgiven by the blood of Jesus, there are consequences for sin. You see… Marcus found out yesterday that he has a son he didn't know about. He's about twenty years old and is a student at the U of Canton. His name is Derek."

I stop for a moment to let that sink in, but Angel looks unfazed by this. I wish I could be. Then she gave a very interesting response, "Well at least he's got a son to get to know now. Whoever this Derek is should be grateful for that." I continue to be amazed at the intelligence of this young woman and want her as a daughter, but we'll see.

****

Later that evening after dinner, I fill Marcus in on the conversation with Angel and the school update. He also lets all of us know at dinner about the meeting today. He's staying away from the council meeting tonight. Right now it's a wait-and-see game. I can tell the weight of the world is on his shoulders. "Millicent, please forgive me for all this," Marcus pleads as we get ready for bed. It's been a very long day. I hold my husband in bed trying to give him strength, even though I'm drained as well. "Marcus. Let's go away after all of this is done." Yep. We need a rest. And we just got back from the Caribbean.

Chapter 14
Marcus
Last Sunday of January

Despite the beginning of the week being chaotic, the rest of the week went okay despite me being nervous about the whole Derek episode, not to mention the Angel situation. Nothing so far on where Big Daddy is, and Sandra seems to think he bolted the state. I'm not so sure. We had Alvin Davis' funeral on Tuesday and it was a packed house. I, of course, avoided Mr. Davis' granddaughter, Morgan at all costs. I didn't realize just how much influence in the business community he had. But the family seemed upset with me for some reason and I don't know why. But they are always that way. *Why couldn't they have turned out like the patriarch of the family?*

On a lighter note, Angel had a good week at school. On Friday we received a call from Principal Margaret saying that she checked in on Angel and her teachers feel like she needs to be in more advanced classes. It's amazing to me how much she has thrived in our home and has settled in like she's one of our own. She appears more comfortable and is into our routine. Jesse came over on a supervised date Friday night. I talked to Greg this week after he returned from Arizona, as Robin's out of town, and we agreed to have supervised dates at each other's houses for now and group situations with the youth at the church, when we get an assistant pastor.   Millicent and Angel went to self-defense class Tuesday evening. I support my wife in her endeavors to help women in our community. She does Bible studies, recently completing one on Proverbs 31. Millicent is an excellent example of a Proverbs 31 wife. Yea and she carries a gun. Some people are put off by that thinking that she's a pastor's wife and should rely on God to protect her. God does protect us, but we also have a choice to be prepared or not. I'm not a gun person myself, but I support her. A point of political discussion for another day.

Wednesday night is youth Bible study at church and that went fairly well. As the church has grown, my workload has increased to the point where I can no longer do everything. I need help. My body feels it and not just from the events of the last week. We had a staff meeting as well and it's further evidence that I need to work on getting an assistant pastor. I'm running myself ragged, coming home every evening so tired. And, I really need to be more attentive at home. To Millie and now to Angel. Yes. I'm complaining. But that part needs to be settled into a better routine when Angel is on one. On the subject of assistant pastor, I called Jared about my idea, and meet with him and a possible candidate. After some checking of references, I believe I am ready to make a decision. That is assuming I'm going to be the pastor. Wednesday was also the funeral for Dr. Brown. It was a private service so I could not attend. I heard not many did. So sad.

Yesterday was a great day. We had a warm January day with highs in the upper 30s and sunny. Millicent had arranged for a few people from the church, including Greg, Robin, and Jesse, to go to the Sarah Moore House and do some demo work. Of course, when she heard that Jesse was going to be there, Angel volunteered to go with my hammer in hand. So we went and we got the wall demo work completed. Next is some electrical and plumbing work. It was a productive day in the house. I had a chance to talk to Greg about life and how the hearings were going about the criminal that terrorized Robin and Jesse a few months ago. "There's no way he'll get off," Greg replied confidently. I then told him about our little problem which was Big Daddy. "Well. It seems the bad guys always like to have a nickname. A very bad one." We laughed. That's the first time in a while I've done that.

****

Sunday has arrived and the schedule will be unusual. I start by preaching the two services. My sermon today in both services is on grace and forgiveness. I hope it sinks in. As usual, the music is extraordinary with Amy and Robin adding strength to the voices of the praise team. I encourage forgiveness as the theme for the music too. And, like most Sundays, Jesse is in the booth, as well as Nathan. Derek has attended both services, sitting in the back row like a lion waiting to devour its prey. The Davises look that way too, though Morgan looks like she wants to devour me for another reason. *Yuck!* I see others as well. Josie is missing, but I assume she's in the nursery and the TV in there broadcasts the services. Others I have sweated with, bled with, and cried with, are there though and I am continuing to be concerned about the business meeting after the second service. *Why do all of the bad things happen at high noon?*

We finally get to the business meeting. I've been on edge for a week. I'm on the stage and Jill has come up. She looks back from the podium, smiles, then turns towards the congregation and opens up with prayer. Then she begins.

"First of all thank you to everyone for coming today. We have a serious matter to discuss and first I want to give Marcus the floor. Marcus?" She surrenders the podium as I begin the speech of my life. I get up and the stand behind the podium, carefully focusing my eyes on my smiling wife and my Angel, then others, and of course my son and my nemesis Derek, looking like he's sitting on a feather. I turn my attention back to the task at hand and so, I take a paper out of the jacket I wore today. Yep. I wore a jacket and tie. I'm serious now. So I begin as I put my game face now. The game of my life.

"Friends. Today I talked about grace and forgiveness. Forgiveness begins with the person who did wrong, then it spreads to others. Today I seek your forgiveness and understanding. In the spirit of openness, I need to make a confession. For those who have been here a long time, you know of my past in college. I was a star linebacker at the University. I had women fall over me. I had pro football prospects. I did whatever I wanted no matter what the consequences were. At that time, I was on top of the world, or so I thought. Then it came crashing down with one injury. God showed me that I was a selfish, young jerk who needed a Savior. So after much prayer from Dr. Porter over there..." I stop and point to my mentor and friend, then continue.

"I came to know our Lord and Savior Jesus Christ. I learned from my new friends, abandoning my old life. Millicent will tell you how I was. She hated me." Some chuckles come from the congregation. "Then, I was fortunate enough to start dating Millicent and the rest is history. I have... I have never broken my marriage vows to Millicent and I want to state that first." I mouth 'I'm sorry' to my Warrior Queen. By now I can see the puzzled stares on people's' faces, people I've cried with, people I rejoiced with for many years. People who will be my judge and jury. But I also glance over at Derek in the back row waiting for the hammer to fall.

"During college, I have not made it a secret that I was a womanizer. I was loose. I did some drugs and alcohol. Yea, I admit it. That's what you do when you feel like you don't need a Savior. Anything I did back then is my responsibility and mine alone. And while God forgives our sins through Jesus, that does not take away the consequences of sin. Now some consequences are blessings. Today, I want to confess that I found out last week that I am a father to an adult son from a past relationship. Before Millicent and I were even dating. And today I have a son who is a blessing to me."

I can hear the gasps and conversations start up. I look over at Millicent and she begins to tear up. This must be tearing her apart. And it rips my heart out I've put her in this position. But despite her tears in her eyes, my lovely bride of fifteen years is smiling at me as if she's encouraging me to have courage. I'm taking some strength from that woman, that rock who will be... no is... a great mother. And, I look at Angel who is taking this all in. I can't imagine how she'll take it being a new Christian if the vote goes south. But I've prayed this week for her to see beyond the negativity. For her sake in whatever happens I need to set the example of faith with her as a new believer. Then I glance at Derek who has a smile on his face. Now I know how David felt with his son Absalom. Because he's my son I have to love him. And I do it willingly. But I hate his heart, yet I have to do this for him too. It's a lesson for all of us on grace. As I peer over the congregation I see the Davises with a smile on my right and the granddaughter gives me a wink. Good Lord! I shake my head in disgust as the crowd dies down so I can continue.

"You know. I've put much prayer and thought into this matter. On the one hand, Jesus talks about forgiveness and leaving a life a sin. Well, I'm a sinner. I admit it. I'm a sinner like everyone here. Can one of you come up here and say truthfully that you are pure? That you have never sinned? That you need forgiveness? Raise your hand if you are perfect?" I stop, obviously to give anyone an opportunity to say so, but I know the answer as they do. "When we sin we should seek forgiveness. Yes, I've asked Millicent and Angel, our new… daughter for forgiveness." I stare with intensity at Angel and she is looking at me with wide, tear-filled eyes. She feels my pain too. Then I go down the steps to the front row with the microphone in hand. I go to Angel, hold her hand and tell her in front of all, "Yes, Angel whatever happens you are a part of our family now." She wipes the tears from her eyes as Millicent holds her. Then I let go and will my eyes to come up to the congregation. "I also publicly ask for the forgiveness of my son. I did not abandon your mother, my son. She left me without letting me know so much as a whisper of your existence. And I have proof. I'm going to read a letter from his mother written over twenty years ago." I pull out the letter I've kept in my college box, along with my college football letter, my other awards, and my souvenirs of days gone by. I don't know why I kept this letter, but I'm glad I did. I pull it out of my pocket, then I pull out my reading glasses, put them on and begin.

Dear Marc -

        These last few months together have been fun. I've enjoyed our time together I guess. I know you told me you loved me but I cannot and don't love you. I hate my life. I hate college, and the more I get closer to you the more I'm afraid I'll fall in love with you. I can't let that happen. You're a good man. A crazy guy, but a good one. But I'm so messed up and tired of everything. I'm leaving school and leaving you. I don't want what you want and can't give what you need. I'm moving away so don't try and find me. I need a new life away from my horrible mom, and away from you, because you're too good for me. Find someone that will be your soulmate.

Take care,
Breanna

I put the letter back in my pocket and look up to see a stunned congregation and on the back row a crying Derek. He's hurt for a long time. But I must finish this.

"Friends. I have been in this church for over ten years. Before that, I was an assistant pastor in Pennsylvania, but I always wanted to come home. Because of this I have been asked to resign and leave the church or else this dirty, little secret would get out."

I stop and let the air go out of the room. Some gasp, others, well, I just not sure how to read them. So I go on.

"If this was a matter of an affair while I was pastor, I would heartily resign. So after an emergency meeting, the ministry board had on Monday night, I have decided to ..." I stop and look at Derek. He's got swollen eyes now but seems to be waiting for my answer, a little too eager for my taste. So I go on again.

"Ask the Board to call a vote of confidence for me today. All members will decide. And I've put the additional challenge to the Board. While they continue to support me, I don't want any doubts. So I'm asking for a 70% vote of confidence, otherwise, we leave. Jill will come up here and run the business meeting while I wait in the office." With that, I take off my reading glasses, put them back in my pocket along with the crumpled letter. Then I get up and leave. As I go, I turn around and glare up at my congregation. God's people. History has shown that believers, while redeemed, don't act like it at times. I hope that's not the case today. But regardless I have resolved to put the matter in God's hands and whatever happens, our family will be taken care of. I want Millicent to remain in the business meeting because I want her to be my eyes and ears. I want Angel to stay as an example, and, since she joined the church last week, she gets a vote.

Chapter 15
Millie

I could not have been more proud of my husband than I am right now. As he leaves I want to chase him down, kiss him like he's never been kissed before, but I know I cannot. Angel is in tears beside me and asks me something, but I 'Shush' her. Jill, my friend for a long time gets up and while the congregation is murmuring and talking among themselves, she and Jared both get up now. They go on the stage and Jill goes to the podium while Jared stands behind her. Then she begins.

"Attention everyone, please. I want to say something. I've known Marcus and Millie for a long time. I know who they were in college and who they are now. When Marcus met with Jared and me last Monday to discuss this he was open and honest about this matter. Frankly, as an attorney and as a believer I abhor blackmail. But that's an issue for another day." She stops then gives a stern, courtroom face in the back to who I assume is Derek. I don't look back there. I focus on Jill. Then she begins again.

"The ministry board went on record in an emergency meeting Monday night to oppose this vote, but Marcus wanted it any way. This was his idea. Not mine. Be warned though. If you vote to ask them to leave today, many will go with him. And I will be one of them."

More murmurs and conversations come from the congregation and then I hear silence. Then, I hear a sound come closer. It's a sound of a... well I'm not sure what it is. It sounds like two sticks hitting together. Click, Click...Click, Click. I look back to see a young woman. A very beautiful

woman coming forward. She is the prettiest woman I
believe I've ever seen. She's about my height, olive skin,
dark, curly flowing hair. looks about twenty or twenty-five
years old. She's walking up one of the aisles. She has on
a purple dress with knee-high boots and a decorative scarf.
She looks stunning. She's also wearing dark glasses and I
notice she has a cane that swings back and forth. Silence
has come across the auditorium. So much so that all
anyone hears is the click of her cane. Then this mystery
woman comes up to the front and faces the crowd. Jill and
Jared are on stage. She turns to Jill and asks, "May I
speak?" Jared quickly gets a spare microphone the
musicians use and gives it to the young woman. Then she
begins in a modest, soft voice, the voice of humility.

"My name is Jasmine Jackson. I... sorry I don't do
crowds usually." Her face is slightly red, and some in the
audience chuckle as she continues. "You don't know me.
And even Pastor Marcus doesn't know me, but I know him.
I just entered the University of Canton this semester to
study for my master's degree in counseling. I start classes
this week. This is my second Sunday here. You see, I
know of Marcus because... my father is in prison. For
robbery. This church cared enough about my father.
Marcus visits the jail here and well... he visits my father
regularly. And while he has a couple of months to go for his
sentence to be finished, Marcus gave him a great gift. A
Bible. You see my father is a believer now because of
Marcus. Well, Jesus used him, but you get the point. But
the story doesn't end there. My mom lives in town and I
went away to school for a while but moved back to take
care of her. You see my mom... we're not well off. So
when my dad asked Marcus to please put our family on the

list to help with Christmas, I am the recipient of many Christmas gifts from the church, including the dress I'm wearing today. But more than that the donor gave money and other things. I didn't know who the donor was until one of the bills had a Mr. Davis' name written on it. Last Sunday I saw that a Mr. Davis had passed, and well, when I went to the registrar on Monday to get my financial aid together, they said a Mr. Davis paid my tuition for the semester. When I pressed the registrar about this, she told me to talk to Pastor Marcus. And well… that's why I came today. You know. If you haven't guessed it I'm blind, physically. But I've been a believer for ten years and I see more clearly today than ever before. Jesus said to the adulterous woman, "Go and sin no more." I'm not a member and I have no vote. But if you get rid of Marcus, then everyone needs to leave because we all fail. But God gives us all grace. And, if He can bless a blind girl, then he can do anything."

With those words that shock the crowd, she takes her cane and leaves the front, stunning the entire place with this revelation.

Murmurs continue in the congregation until Jill calls for order. Then Jared leans over to Jill and whispers something, and the Jill turns back toward the front and tells everyone, "Jared has asked to speak." She surrenders the podium to Jared who begins.

"Ladies and gentlemen. In full disclosure, I talked with Marcus last Sunday afternoon about this issue as he was more than open to share everything. This was only a couple of hours after he was made aware that he had a son. Folks, let me first say that we should honor the fact that he's not abandoning his responsibility to his son. I know that

Marcus would have wished he would've known about his son, who he was, and what he needed and wanted. But others made decisions for him and kept him in the dark. I frankly have made mistakes in the past. I'm not a perfect person in life either, but who is? Who among you is perfect? If you are, step forward." Jared stops for a pregnant pause, then goes on. "I can understand if Marcus was having an affair while pastor that would be a problem. Pastors should be an example for others. And what an example he's set. Without Marcus we would have no jail ministry, no battered women's ministry, no addictions ministry, shall I list others? Marcus has led us to support various missionaries, has worked on houses in the area, marriage retreats, financial planning, youth, young adults. Millie leads self-defense classes and women's singles retreats. And all of this with little staff support because we won't help him. Well, it's time for this church to decide what to do. If you decide to vote no confidence in your pastor, then this church will be moving backward, and you can count on me…" He stops and looks over at his family and as I quickly glance over there they are all nodding yes as a united family should. Well, Ellis isn't. He's asleep in Charlotte's arms. I turn my attention back to Jared as he finishes up by saying, "my entire family supports Marcus and Millie and well… If you decide to ask them to leave, then we will too. And I'm not saying that because I want Marcus to be here forever. No one person is a church. Marcus is here at the right time and at the right place. And a no vote is going against God." More murmurs come out and as Jared leaves the podium and goes to sit with his family.

"Okay. It's time to vote. Since this comes from the

ministry board, even though they object to it, it does not need a motion or second. Board members have been organized to count. And, Remember if you're not a member you cannot vote. All those in favor signify by raising your right hand."

Angel and I raise our right hand and I cannot bare to watch anyone else. I really don't have a feeling as to how this will go. Then quickly Jill says "okay." All those opposed to Marcus staying as pastor raise your right hand. A moment passes and I close my eyes. This is the moment that will define our lives. I close my eyes, then I hear applause, and awaken from my thoughts, then Angel turns to me and whispers, "we stay!" How can that be? The vote was too quick! Jill then says meeting adjourned and everyone starts to file out. I'm stunned. We are still here, but for how long? How close was the vote? Jill then comes down to Angel and me and says, "Millie let's go tell Marcus the good news." I start to ask how the vote went but I'm still in shock as to how it took so little time to count and what the count actually was. A church split comes to mind as I fear for the worst.

As we float our way back to Marcus' office, I can barely move my feet. I open my husband's door and see him in prayer on his knees at his desk. This is the man I married. Humble, yet handsome. He risked it all. "The vote's over Marcus. You're still here if you want it, though for God only knows why." I chuckle at Jill's declaration. She's my close friend and I am in total shock to her calmness and her demeanor. My heart is still in my throat.

"How was the vote?" Marcus asks as his eyes come up from the desk. He appears haggard. These past events have definitely taken their toll.

"You had almost everyone support you. There were five no votes, all from one family - the Davises. But the granddaughter apparently likes you and she voted 'yes' much to the dismay of her family. But what really swung the vote I believe was a young woman named Jasmine. Do you know her?"

Marcus smiles and chuckles a little bit. Then replies, "No I don't know her. Should I?"

I reply, "Well, she apparently knows of you as Mr. Davis paid for her schooling and she said something about you delivering an envelope to the financial aid office and well... I'm not sure the whole story."

"I may know something about that," Jill interrupts. "I do have another duty to perform. Marcus. You as the church's pastor and Millie as the director of the women's shelter are legally compelled to be in my office tomorrow morning at 10 am along with the Davis family. Mr. Davis' will is being read and the Church and you both are named in it. And Millie? As co-chair of the Revitalization Association of Canton, I'll need backup too?"

"Uh... Okay? So anything I need to know about?"

"Sorry Marcus. You'll have to wait until tomorrow. Oh, and Jasmine will be there too. You get to have a ringside seat to the circus that is all things Davis. Oh and one more thing. I have some... connections with the courts and with some people over Josie. Josie is doing a fine job but her powers are limited. So I've arranged for you to have permanent custody and when that creep is caught, you get a chance to adopt Angel, if you want." With that Jill waves and leaves the office leaving a tornado in her wake.

Marcus gets up goes from his desk and hugs Angel and me. Things are looking up for our little family. Then

Marcus releases our hug and tells both of us, "I need to reconcile with my son or at least try. He's lost, but he's still my son. And, I'm still responsible. Is it okay that I go see him later today after we stop for lunch and I will try to engage him at the University. Fortunately, I still have some pull with the football team." He certainly does. No one mentioned it earlier but Marcus also volunteers with the football team as the team's chaplain. Yea we stay busy, but with Angel, our priorities need to change. It's clear today that Marcus needs help and with Jared's encouragement, maybe that'll happen sooner than later.

Chapter 16
Marcus

Seeing my son's tears in his eyes as I read Breanna's letter was hard. It broke my heart to do it this way. I didn't want to do that but I little choice. And it gave me a sense of closure with that chapter in my life. Reconciliation works two ways. If my son wants a relationship with me, then I will gladly hold my hand out. But if he doesn't I'll wait. Even though my relationship with Breanna was wrong on so many levels, the blessing was my son. He just doesn't know it yet. So after lunch with Angel and Millie, I text Coach Clark asking where Derek lives and he sends me the information. I then take them home and go over to the University of Canton. I make my way to Dugger Hall, the male dorm where most of the football players stay. Earlier in the week , I talked to Coach Clark to find out more about Derek. He's a junior college transfer from Florida. He's cocky but a good prospect and is a safety for the Canton Cavaliers football team. **Go Cavaliers!** I'm told he's a fair student but could do better. Everybody's telling me information off-the-record. Right now he's a finance major. He lives in Room 207 in Dugger Hall. Armed with new insight into some things about Derek, I make my way to the dorm. As I enter the dorm using the pass code I received form the administration, a pungent smell hits my nostrils. Dugger Hall still smells like a locker room the same way it did twenty years ago. I go up the stairs to Room 207. Funny. I was in 205 for a year. I knock on the door. After a shuffle for a second, the door swings open and I find myself face-to-face with my younger self. Derek gives a snort and blurts out, "What do you want!"

"Well, hello to you too. I came to talk."

Derek leaves the door open and I go in. I didn't wait to be invited. I want in, say my peace, then make an escape in case he slugs me.

"How did you know where I live?" He asks.

"Oh. Well, in case you haven't heard I've been the team chaplain for about five years now. I have my ways." I quickly scan around the room. It still has a few boxes. The bed is unmade. Typical males college room and smell.

"Ugh" was all I got as he turned away from me and faces the window.

"Listen, Derek. I know you're hurting and I'd like to help you, but blackmailing me is not the way." That got his attention as he faces me and I saw something...*Fear?* Then he sits on his bed. So I continue.

"Derek I want to be your father. I can't make up for lost time, and I can't make it up to your mother. By the way where is she? I never asked?"

"She died. Last year of breast cancer," he squeaks as his voice cracks.

"I'm sorry Derek. I'm sorry about your mother." I truly am. Nothing could change the past, but maybe the future can be better for him and for me.

"I wish I could change things but I can't. But I'd be willing to answer any questions you have about your mother and me. And I may have a few pictures of her. I saved a lot as you noticed. Would you come over to dinner at my house tomorrow, say 5:00? We can privately talk. Then we can have dinner. Millicent... well... let's just say that I'll get us some good food. I promise that."

I see a small, very small smile briefly go on Derek's

face. Maybe I've cracked the wall. Food is a good motivator for a hungry college football player.

He looks back at the window facing the quad. Sunlight filters into the room as he seems to be contemplating my invitation. Then Derek turns his head back to me, points at me, and replies, "Okay... 5:00, but the food better be good." So I give him directions to my house and maybe the ice age has ended with my son. So I turn to leave. Just then, Derek asks me a strange question. "Who is Jasmine?"

"I don't know yet. But I find out tomorrow morning. I have a meeting about her, and a will." Derek raises his eyebrow as I make my way to the door. We aren't at the hugging stage yet but we at least are pleasant enough to say goodbye to each other and be civil.

On the drive back home I replay the conversation and the day. Just like Angel my son needs a Savior. Maybe tomorrow night begins that journey with him. As I pull onto my street I notice the regular patrol of the Canton PD and I notice a black SUV sitting down the street that seems out of place. *Must be a guest of Mavis'.*

I stop my car in the driveway and praise God for the day. It's been very hard and I really need to get some rest, both physically and emotionally. I get out and go into the house. As I enter I see Angel and Millicent at the island working on Angel's homework. I take a hard look at my family. In such a short period of time, our two has grown to three. Then it hits me. It's now four if Derek wants to be a part of it. Angel gets up and comes over to me and gives me a bear hug. *I could get used to this.* But probably next year she'll hate me. Millicent comes over. Then she gives me a kiss. 'I've been neglecting her,' my inner voice speaks to my heart. "I want you both to know that I love you," I say out loud so they both know my true feelings. Then we all go in for the group hug like on those 1960s family TV shows.

****

During dinner, I let Angel and Millicent know that I invited Derek to dinner tomorrow night and asked my wife if she can get Sofia to make something. She agreed, chuckling and knowing that she can't cook. A person has to know his or her limitations, right? But, I never complain, because I know that can only lead to certain death or at least a horrific argument. Maybe that wouldn't be so bad. Arguments eventually lead to making up, right? I also remind them that we've been called to Jill's office tomorrow morning to hear the reading of the will for Mr. Davis and Jasmine is a part of it. I have asked Millicent to ride with me. I need the support. My wife whispers over to me, and tells me, "It's time to have a talk with Angel." So I speak up to Angel, "Uh. Angel? When we're finished with dinner, can we have a family discussion in the living room? You're not in trouble but we feel like we need to talk about a few things." She says, "okay" reluctantly, then clears the dishes, washes them and heads to the living room where we have made our way to relax a bit.

"So, Angel, we need to have a talk about some ground rules and also to guide you as a new believer. Do you understand?"

"Yes, but Marcus, I haven't done anything wrong. If I have let me know and I'll fix it. I..."

"Angel. Stop. Listen to me before you start drawing conclusions." She seems to relax a bit and while we sit across from her Millicent begins.

"Angel. Honey. We want to let you know that we love you. And, we're working on trying to keeping you forever and being our daughter. I'm getting Jill McDaniels, our attorney involved and whatever it takes you will be with us. We're doing all we can."

****

Today is Monday again, and as we've reached the end of January, these last few weeks and even months have been, to say the least, exciting, scary and challenging. After my prayers for the day, I head to the gym, and to the staff meeting. I've been praying for help at the church and, well, I may have finally concluded who the new assistant pastor should be, that is if he accepts. I'm going on faith here, so it'll be interesting.

Chapter 17
Millie

Going to Jill's office should be good because she's a great friend and I've known her for a long time. But this morning is official and I feel like I'm headed to court for a traffic ticket. Marcus postponed the staff meeting this morning until Wednesday as he and I are headed into the law office. We stop at the entrance and as he holds my hand, he stares at me invading my soul with those gorgeous eyes. He is very handsome in his suit and paisley tie. So. Very. Handsome. He kisses me on the cheek then whispers, "Ready darling?" We really need to get some alone time. I nod 'yes' like a schoolgirl and we go in. We walk to the elevator and get in.   It takes us to the third floor as the typical boring elevator music plays. When the ding goes off indicating we arrived, the door opens and we step out only to be greeted by the office receptionist Rella McKnight. Rella goes to the same church as Margaret, but her son comes to some for the Freedom Church activities. She has a teenage son with learning disabilities and struggles to be a single parent.

"Hey Rella," I say smiling, with my husband at my side. Marcus releases my hand and shakes hers. "Millie, Marcus. Glad to see it all worked out yesterday. You're on time. Everyone's in the conference room down the hall. We're waiting on Jasmine and Iris Jackson. She should be here in…" At that moment the elevator dings and Jasmine steps off with an older woman who likes a lot like her. Jasmine says, "Hello. We here for our 10 o'clock?"

I say, "Hello Jasmine," then put out my hand moving it to her to shake it. She stops and gets closer, then she smells me? Then she steps back towards the other woman, then tells us, "Is a man with you I smell a cologne I'm not familiar with?" Marcus quickly puts his hand out and introduces himself. "I'm Marcus and it seems I owe you a lot for yesterday. If there's anything I can do for you let me know." Jasmine replies, "Big hand." We all chuckle, then Jasmine moves her head towards the woman beside her and introduces her as her "mom". Her name is Iris. Jill comes out of the conference room and then motions for us to come in. And, I wave at Rella as we move in the room.

When we enter, I notice the five members of the Davis family sitting at the table, another person who looks like a clerk or something in the back. Jill declares, "Why don't you all have a seat and we'll get started." The sons of Mr. Davis look like they want to kill us. This should be interesting. As we get seated Jill begins.

"In my capacity as the late Alvin Davis' attorney and his executor I am obligated to meet with all parties involved in the execution of his final wishes as outlined in his will. I will provide copies later but I want to make some things very clear. For the record all parties required are present. Mr. Davis and I met eight months ago to rework his will."

Collective gasps come from the Davis family. Then Jill interrupts and tells us, "Listen. He made his desires very specific and very clear. So I'm going to summarize his will then you can read it yourself. I also have a video to show you. The will requires everyone available to watch it or any inheritance is lost."

Jill takes a stapled stack of paper out of a file on the table in front of her and begins to read:

"To his two sons, Ivan and Sherman you will each get the house, most of Mrs Davis' physical possessions, and the proceeds of a life insurance policy to be divided equally. All estimated to total about two million dollars which will be divided equally."

I peer quickly over at the Davis' and they don't have a happy face on, except the granddaughter who keeps looking at Marcus. Oh brother.

"To his only grandchild Morgan, you will receive a trust fund in the amount of $350,000 when you reach the age of 30 or have been married for at least two years or have been married and have a child. Any of your offspring up to three children will have a fund as well. You also receive immediately his cabin near Sugarcreek."

I take a short but quick glance over at her and she looks puzzled. Hmm.

"Now to the bulk of the estate. Mr. Davis was a very wealthy man but didn't show it. He lived in a three-bedroom house that the family grew up in and was very generous with his money, giving a lot away in secret. He, therefore, has declared the following:

The Freedom Church will get 16.345 million dollars and will be divided as follows:

The Sarah Moore House will receive 2 million dollars in memory of his wife Marilyn to go towards helping the project get started and to help battered women or homeless pregnant women. He wanted me to say that Marilyn was treated badly by her father and would have wanted this project is she was alive today.

A scholarship funding the amount of 6 million dollars will be set up for the less fortunate members of church families who need help with college. Priority is given to members of the church staff including the pastor and his family should he adopt or foster any children. And the

Moore family in memory of Sarah."

Marcus and I stare at each other in shock and glee. My first thought is Angel. But Jill plows on.

"Eligibility will be determined by merit and by a committee appointed by the church.

1.5 million is to be established as a fund to develop a prison ministry for the local jail and surrounding prisons and work farms. This fund may be used for salaries.

Five million dollars goes into the church building fund and will be used to build a gymnasium or multi-purpose space to house church-sponsored athletic events. A ball field will also be procured near the church with these funds.

The remainder goes into the preschool ministry in memory of his daughter Elle who died at age three when she fell down the stairs. The program shall establish scholarships with half of the money to go to those who need childcare based on need as determined by fair income standards established by the church."

A sigh comes from the Davis family and silence covers the room, until the eldest Davis, whose name is Ivan, gets up and starts to talk, then Jill holds out her hand to indicate 'stop', interrupts once again and instructs him, "I'm not finished so sit down!"

Silence enters the room again as he slowly complies with the Jill I know.

"The Revitalization Association of Canton is represented by co-chair Mrs. Millicent Jenkins. The elder Mr. Davis, through his generosity, loaned out to small businesses money he started to get up and be sustainable. This was through the association he started and was secretly behind all these years. Some businesses include ZON Studios, a couple of bed and breakfasts, and the like.

The total loans outstanding at the time of Alvin's death amounted to about $850,000. He stated that any businesses at the time of his death who had an outstanding loan through the association would have their loans forgiven and the money be paid through his will." At least the Moore boys will be happy.

"To Iris Jackson, Alvin left you a trust fund with an annual dispensing of $50,000 for ten years with the remainder going in the eleventh unless you are married with the remainder going to you immediately. To Jasmine Jackson. A scholarship has been established at the University of Canton to pay for your entire education, textbooks, and any living expenses. You will also receive $50,000 for ten years with the remainder going in the eleventh year unless you are married then the remainder will go immediately to you like your mother. He said he really appreciates you Iris for taking care of him during his last months. If you pass away before the eleven years expire the remainder of the trust will go in total to Jasmine. Honey, he never met you but admired you from afar because of your courage, beauty, and strength. His wishes were for you to pursue a doctorate and there is funding to do so."

Murmurs go throughout the room. Then Ivan gets up and tells the entire room while pointing to Jill. "This will not stand! We will fight this!" The Davises get louder until Jill uses her courtroom voice and tells everyone to sit down and there's more.

"I have been instructed to show a video and to let you know more at the end."

The room lights dim as the clerk has gotten up and gone to the computer. The projector in the room lights up and a blue hue lights up, then a video of Alvin Davis comes on. He appears fine. It's hard to believe he's dead but he's with Jesus now. I know that.

"Dear family and others. I know my time is limited and I've not got much longer to live. I changed my will to give my earthly possessions to those who needed it. To my sons. My biggest regret in life is that you never got to know Jesus as I did. Your mother and I raised you to know him yet when you made your own money and when we gave you all you could ever want and need, you still felt like it wasn't enough. From the grave, I urge you one more time to accept Jesus. We want to see you again." Mr. Davis stops and wipes his face as tears flow down his checks then he continues.

"To my granddaughter, Morgan. You are my only grandchild and probably will be my only grandchild because of the selfishness of my sons. And that selfishness has rubbed off on you. It has not gone unnoticed that you chase after older men you can't have and flaunt yourself. Child, I urge you to change your ways before it's too late. Find a decent guy to marry, but focus on changing yourself first. Take a hard look at yourself in the mirror and deep down in your heart. Get right with God and he will provide you a great man. A man that probably won't be rich, that won't be the most handsome, but will be loyal and trustworthy and has a heart of gold. But again, you may be surprised. And, you won't have to worry about who he's with, like your mother and father. Adultery has been a cancer on your life. So to get away from it, I gave you the cabin so you can enjoy it with your future family. I hope you keep it. It's your choice. I would suggest you move in it a while to get away from your mother and father and think about these things.

Get a job away from your father and focus on serving others, not your own selfishness. Millie and Jill will help you in that area. You're going to have a degree. Use it or go back to school or get a job to help others. But above all get right with God. When you find a guy make sure he's a Christian and make sure he takes care of you. And take care of him like your grandmother did for me. Millie can help you in these things. Seek her Godly wisdom and advice." All eyes are now on Morgan who is very embarrassed and is very red, like a tomato. Then I turn my attention back to the screen.

"To my family, I say these things in desperate love. Whether you listen or not is up to you. Now to Marcus and Millie my good friends and my pastors. Don't think I haven't noticed your good work here in Canton to make it a better place. You both struggle and scrape but that has made you stronger. Please go get that family through adoption or other means. I have been told I cannot require it but I have provided Jill with sufficient funds to handle the legal process for two adoptions for you in addition to her fee for handling my estate. Please be the parents I know you will be. As for the church, I know you have so many projects to help the community and I want to bless those, but I also do not want the church to get lazy and not provide for the regular funds, so I've stated that none of my memorial funds be used for regular expenses including personnel costs. The only exception is the prison ministry." I look at Marcus knowing we're both think the same thing. Angel could be ours.

"Iris. Thank you so much for being more than my in-home care nurse. In addition to taking care of me, you took the time to tell me about you, your daughter and your husband who's in jail. You never knew about my money and had no motivation to be a friend other than being a good person and a believer in Jesus. And, you became a true friend and angel that I needed in a short amount of time. Jasmine. I've never met you, but the Lord place it on my heart to help you. For some reason, he has told me that you will be incredibly blessed soon by a gentleman and will need to help him find his way. He will also help you in a desperate time of need in your life. Trouble is coming, but blessings will be after it. Be open to friendships and even romance, but also be wise like I know you are. Your mother says you are brilliant. For someone who's blind physically, you see better than most people with your heart, or so your mother says.

Finally, I know that the changes in my will probably cause a few in my family to question my sanity. You can try. But there will be a price for challenging my will in court. I have directed my attorney to put in a clause that anyone who legally challenges my will or manipulates my desires in any way through legal or other means, will forfeit all of the provisions. And before each person leaves today he or she must sign a waiver to legally challenge the will. Otherwise no money. No nothing. Take care and I pray I see you again in heaven alongside with my wife and my Elle. Consider my words carefully."

The video goes black and the lights come up in the room. I take in everyone's faces and I see the shock on all. My face probably feels the heat from the blush of my cheeks. I didn't know Alvin Davis was filthy rich. But he was smart. I'll give him that. Then Jill clears her throat to gain the attention of the attendees and barks out, "Okay. Copies of the will are to be distributed by my clerk. I can assure you that it's challenge-proof. I had four doctors to examine him for competency and have all certified he was fit to make this will. I also have closed every other challenge loophole. As you glance at it and read your copy of the will, you can take it with you. Before you leave, you must sign a copy of the waiver which is attached to the back of your copy of the will. Now one other thing. Once you leave this room no one is allowed to discuss the will provisions with each other or anyone outside of this room. Alvin gave me strict instructions of who you can discuss it with. And that list is very small. And those people have to sign a disclosure as well. Violations of the will mean forfeiture of the terms." Jill then gets up as the clerk passes around copies. I do not hesitate. I turn to the back, tear off the last sheet and sign under my name. It looks like Marcus, Iris, and Jasmine do the same thing. I'm awakened from my thoughts when Ivan stands and announces, "He's thought of everything hasn't he? That old coot. I hate him."

Jill was now very angry and she retorts, "Ivan, he loved all of you. You just didn't love him so he did what he hoped would be best for everyone. Besides, you don't need the money anyway. Stop acting like that."

"You know that means our family will no longer use you as our attorney," Sherman replies in defense of his brother.

Jill laughs, then laughs some more holding her tummy. I don't think I've ever seen her laugh so hard. Finally, she informs them all, "I don't need your business you idiots. Sorry, Marcus. Once you sign the forms then I will make sure you don't step in these offices again."

Both the Davis men glance at each other, while Morgan looks like she's mulling the offer. They don't seem to notice Morgan at all or even care about her. Poor

Morgan. Despite all she's done tormenting my husband with her innuendos, she's to be pitied. Morgan's father Ivan, has never paid attention to the precious child he has. Lost, but precious. As I watch Morgan, her hands are shaking and tears form in her eyes. She's so lost and even though I should be angry for her advances to Marcus, I'm secure enough in our marriage to know my gorgeous husband would never, ever step out, especially with that child. Then Morgan turns to the last page and signs the paper. She gets up as her father and uncle pay her no mind. Morgan comes over to Jasmine who is sitting beside me and takes her hand gently and says, "Jasmine. I'm Morgan and I'd like to get to know you."

        "I'd like that very much." They release each other's hands and Morgan moves to me. "Millie. I'm sorry. Can I set up an appointment? I'd like to talk about some… things." I nod then Morgan leaves as we contemplate our next move.

                        ****

        After a few minutes of conversations, the Davis men sign their forms, get up, and leave quietly. Yeah, we stay. I really wanted to see what they would do. My curiosity is a weakness of mine. Marcus leans over to Jill and says to her, "Can you work on Angel's case and get back with us?" "Already on it" was her reply. Then the rest of us get ready to leave. We say goodbye to Jill then outside of the conference room we tell Rella goodbye, then push the button for the elevator. On the elevator, Marcus looks at me and as if he's reading my mind, he invites Iris and Jasmine to lunch.

At lunch in the Roman Cafe on campus, we sit enjoying our lunch, getting to know our new friends. So we all go to get to know one another. As we do I've come to have a high regard for Jasmine and her mom. Jasmine is a force of nature, just like her mother. They tell me about Joe, Jasmine's father, and I see Marcus making a note on his phone to go see him again. It's great news that he's due out in about two months and while he's been in, Joe finished a college degree in general studies. I hope someone will give him a chance. As we sit there I notice Derek approaching our table. He has a hopeful facial expression as he can't seem to take his eyes off of Jasmine. Mmm. Marcus notices him, stands up and greets him. "Derek. Doing okay?" He nods his head as he still is glaring at Jasmine as if he's in some hypnotic state. I can't help but chuckle as Iris' eye twitches in amusement. Marcus coughs a little and tells the group, "Jasmine, Iris? This is my son Derek." Derek shakes Iris' hand gently then eyes Jasmine like a cat ready to eat a bird. Then he gently shakes her hand. Now Jasmine does not know that Derek is the one that tried to blackmail Marcus. So her reaction is pleasant, smiling and saying to Marcus' son, "nice to meet you, Derek." Then she does something odd. *She smells him?*

"Uh... Derek. 5:00 right?" As if he's coming out of a dream, Derek responds, "Yea, sure. 5:00." We are there a moment then Derek quickly glances at his watch and starts to dart off saying, "Sorry class in five minutes. Gotta go." And just like that, he's gone. After the morning we had, a good chuckle is needed. I hate to say this but Jasmine is too good for Derek but I hold that thought to myself. I bet Marcus is thinking the same thing though.

Chapter 18
Marcus

This morning and lunch were entertaining and enlightening at the very least. Mr. Davis was a good man and today demonstrated that he really loved the church. I am shocked and truly in awe of the blessings the church will receive. Nevertheless, Mr. Davis' will presents an even greater challenge to add staff and to do more in the community. Lunch with Jasmine and Iris was entertaining with Derek in obvious lust over Jasmine. That child is very pretty, and I think that not only Derek could not keep his eyes off of her but every male college student, and even some professors, have taken several glances. Her blindness to me only enhances her beauty as well as her heart. I'm intrigued by Mr. Davis' comments on the video about Jasmine. *Who is this mystery person?* It seems lately we have more and more mysteries to unravel.

After lunch, Millicent and I decide to head home. We notice our usual police car on the corner, and as I look down the street I still see the black SUV that's been there near Mavis' house for a few days off and on. *Do Charlotte and Kyle have a new vehicle?* Tomorrow when I go to the church I'll be sure to ask Charlotte and Mavis, if she's there. It's about 2:00 and we have about two hours or so before Angel gets home. She's been riding the bus and the stop is next to our house. The officer has been kind enough to escort her to the door. Kudos to the Canton PD. I know police get a bad rap, and any occupation has a couple of bad apples, even clergy. But we've had nothing but positive experiences with the Canton PD, the Sheriff's Office, and federal law enforcement. Millicent's hometown in West

Virginia is the only place we've not had a great experience in. It's small and the town department may have four employees. The chief has it in for Millicent, because she... dated his son in high school and they broke up. We went one time and he stopped us for nothing. So we try to avoid that situation if possible. But that's a story for another day.

As we get to the door, I lean over to her and say, "We have two hours. Want to... play?" That's my code word for making love. Another code word is *exercise* or some other innuendo. Hey, I'm a guy. I didn't lose my sex drive when I became a pastor. Or nearing forty. Millicent gives me her seductive smile, puts her arms around my neck and kisses me hard. Then she opens the door, and says, "Last one to the bedroom has to do the dishes tonight." Then she takes off. Cheater.

****

As we're lying in bed, after a fun time, I glance over at the clock and it's about thirty minutes before Angel gets home. I can hear and feel Millicent breathe as she has her head on my bare chest. Her short hair is messy, but a fun messy. I gaze at Millicent, and she tells me, "When all of this happened with Derek, I was angry. Not necessarily at you but him. For how he let you know about him. And, I admit I was very jealous of Breanna because she... She has something I will never get with you and that is a child. Then we found out she had died, I felt numb. Just numb. I guess I need to find my role in this new family situation. And to throw in Angel in all of this is a bit overwhelming. And, I see how you have agonized over everything. I know our marriage is strong, but..."

She tapers off and I really have no words, except, "I'm truly sorry for all of this. I wish I could change everything but I can't."

"Marcus. You've said you're sorry plenty of times and I'm not really looking for that anymore. I guess all of these changes at once are a bit overwhelming."

"I don't ever want you to think you are not enough for me. With or without a child, you are as beautiful and as precious to me as the moment I fell in love with you. No. Even more special. Most women would have run for the hills after the last two weeks, but you haven't."

A little more silence fills the room as we lay there taking in our words. "Marcus? How do you think dinner's going to go tonight?"

"Don't know but it won't be dull."

"Well. It's time to get dressed before Angel gets home."

I exhale knowing she's right but I could stay here for a long time. But that's not to be. So we get up and get dressed, go to the bathroom and comb our hair so we don't look like we rolled off the bed, which we do, and as we finish, Angel walks in the front door.

Chapter 19
Millie

An afternoon with Marcus was just what I needed to make it through the rest of the day because we need that connection. Marcus and I have a special connection that goes beyond the physical. It is a heart, mind and soul connection that, while Christ-centered, is a unique bond that is sometimes indescribable. On most days, we know each other's thoughts and how each other feels without even verbalizing it. It's just a feeling of human completeness that I've never had with anyone before. And Marcus feels the same. I know it.

As Angel comes in the door, I ask how her day was and she said it was 'fine', a typical teenager response. But for her, normality is good. I remind her that Derek is to be here soon and then I'm honest with her. I don't quite know how it's going to go. The doorbell rings and I answer it. I open the door to a somewhat pregnant Sofia, a couple of grocery bags, and the smell of something... Oh, I can't quite make it out but it smells too delicious for my taste buds.

"*Buenas tardes a todos*," Sofia says in Spanish, which means 'Good afternoon everybody' I think. I don't know Spanish very well.

"Come in darling," I say as the smell of great food permeates the room. Marcus comes over, almost leaping over the couch to take the food to the kitchen. Excited much? "Thanks, Marcus," Sofia adds with a giggle. She is so fun and energetic. I love her.

"Ángel? How are you doing? You look really good or as we say *realmente bueno*." Now Angel gets all smiley and Sofia hugs her. Hard! Sofia releases her hug affair with Angel and turns to Millie. "Now Millie, this is baked spaghetti squash. It's still warm but put in the oven for about ten minutes covered on 300 then turn the oven off and leave it in until you are ready. The sauce is homemade and I added a little kick to it." She giggles and she just hums along. Fast talker. "There's also homemade Italian bread with an olive oil dip and the Caesar salad is in there with my homemade dressing. Finally and what for it... Dah. Dah. Daaah. Nathan's homemade tiramisu. It is gooood." Now I'm hungry. Marcus comes back from the kitchen with wide eyes as if he's ready to eat now. Not gonna happen.

"Sofia? Tell Nathan thanks and we can't thank you enough for this. We'll return your containers."

"Thanks Millie. One more thing. Ángel? I was wondering if you may want a small part-time job at the preschool to clean up after you get out of school. We need someone to do that and I have it in the budget to hire for an hour or so every day. Interested? That is of course if Millie and Marcus agree."

Now Angel's face shines bright with that smile. I'm not opposed to it but we probably need to discuss as a family. As if she knows what I'm thinking Angel tells Sofia, "Oh Mrs. Moore I'd be happy to but we will probably need to discuss it first and with my situation in uh... unknown, I want to be available."

Sofia laughs. "I still can't get used to being called 'Mrs. Moore'. Okay, think about it and let me know. Well I have to go. Nick is coming for dinner and well maybe Josie too."

Nick and Josie? Hmm. They both have baggage.

But interesting thought. He's a little old for her but maturity is not a bad thing and Josie, while she has her hangups, is very mature for her age. Mmm. I hope I didn't say my thoughts out loud, as I look around it seems I didn't. Good.

We hug Sofia, and as she leaves I ask how she's feeling, being that she's halfway through her pregnancy. "Oh, Millie I couldn't tell you how sick I was. Puked everywhere, but now I feel really good. We find out the sex soon and we're doing some tests to determine the baby's health. Just to be sure. By the way. Did you hear the news? About Charlotte and Kyle?"

Worry comes on me. They've been through a lot. Sofia goes on to say, "Because of Charlotte's health, you know she can't have any more children, but they're looking into adoption. Maybe overseas or even foster, like you. I think it's exciting. Well gotta run. *Nos vemos más tarde.*" Sofia leans in, gives me a hug, and she takes off as fast as she came. *What did she say?*

I go back in and close the door, looking at the clock and Derek is due in a few minutes. I look out the window to see the cop still parked across the street. Maybe they'll find him soon. "Honey?" Marcus' voice brings me out of my thoughts. "Yea?"

"I keep seeing an SUV parked near Mavis' and I don't recognize it. Is it Charlotte's?"

"Don't know. I have to go tomorrow to the preschool. What me to ask?"

"Sure. Thanks." Marcus says as Angel returns from the kitchen.

"Millie? I have homework. Can I go and do it before we have our company?" What a good girl.

"Sure Angel. I'll call you when it's time. Okay?"

And she goes.

****

A while later right at 5:00 the doorbell rings and Marcus goes to get it. As for me, I'm nervous as heck and go with him. Then I remember I have my gun on my back waist. Oh well, I'll put it up later. Marcus opens the door and greets Derek with a handshake. And so it begins.

Chapter 20
Marcus

As I open the door it's as if I'm looking at a younger version of myself. Some differences, but very much the same. I put out my hand for him to shake, and he returns it firmly. I invite my son in. Now, I have to remember that despite his deception, he's still my son, and also because he's a nonbeliever he doesn't know how to be a good neighbor in the Biblical sense. We go into the living room, and I formally introduce him to my wife. "This is my wife Millicent. Millicent? Derek." They both shake hands and the awkwardness is evident. Guess who came to dinner. I offer a seat in the living room and my Warrior Queen sits beside me on the couch, while Derek sits across from us. We stare at each other for a minute, then Millicent says, "Derek? You'll be happy for dinner tonight I hope. It's Spaghetti Squash with homemade sauce and tiramisu for dessert. I wish I could take credit for the meal but some friends helped us."

"Sounds good but I've never had tiramisu. What is it?"

"Do you like coffee?" Millicent asks.

"Yea. I drink it all the time."

"Then you'll like this dessert. I going to go check on dinner. Marcus? Why don't you go into the office. Derek may want to see some things." I see her leave and can't help staring at my beautiful bride's backside. But...

"Let's go," I tell Derek and we both get up as he follows me to the office off of the master suite. Now yesterday I pulled out some things that may be of interest to Derek. I don't know how much he wants to know but I decided to take his lead on that. We go into the office where we sit.

After a moment, Derek puts his head in his hands and says, "This is awkward isn't it." I chuckle, trying to lighten the mood and reply, "Yea a bit, but Derek I don't want it to be. Tell me what you want to know and I'll share what I can."

"Well, when I heard the letter I was shocked. It sounded like my mom, but I just cannot believe she lied to me over these years. She told me she never knew who my father was, then said she met him.. I mean you in college. Her story changed with every passing year until I just stopped asking. Then, I found a couple of letters from you after she died and put two and two together and well when I saw your picture online I knew. I just knew."

"Derek? I wish I did know that you existed. I've wanted children. Millicent and I have wanted children but we can't have any."

Derek interrupts and says skeptically, "But you told me you have a daughter."

"Yea. That's complicated. We took custody of Angel less than two weeks ago. She's not technically ours in the sense of adoption, but we do have temporary custody for now. And we hope to adopt her soon. But she's great. You'll meet her for dinner."

"I think I saw her at church," Derek replies as he gazes at me as if he's trying to determine if I am telling the truth. I can understand that. He must be really skeptical of things. He's going to be a tough nut to crack.

"So what can you tell me about my mom?" Derek asks. So I tell him what I know. I go over everything leaving nothing out. Then I add, "Derek, I have some things here. Letters returned unopened, pictures, everything I have on your mother. I don't know why I saved them. I just did." I get up and go over to the box on the other chair and get out things for him. He looks over my shoulder and into the box. Snoop. He then sees my college letters and other awards. My All-American letter and the like.

"You know yesterday when I went to the Bronski Athletic Center I saw your name in the Cavalier Sports Hall of Fame. I didn't know you were the sack leader for the conference and an All-American. That's pretty awesome. Why don't you hang these things up? Why keep them in a box? They're pretty special. I'd have a big trophy case or something."

I'm not sure I should call him 'son' yet but I wish I could. So instead I simply explain what's on my heart. "I loved football. More than just about anything. I was scouted by the professionals. I had everything I could in the world. I could have had money, I had fame, played on national TV. But I also had other things that I wish I could take back. After your mother left I buried myself in football, women, booze, anything that could make me what I thought was happy. But I really wasn't. I lost it all when I became injured. All of the things I had depended on to ensure my so-called happiness was destroyed with one hit. It wasn't until I gave myself over to Jesus that I found real happiness and joy. I'm not scared of dying, I'm not scared anymore. Is my life always happy? No. But it's always joyful. And joy is everlasting, while happiness can fade and sometimes can be an illusion. Someday you'll want a wife and family. Priorities change."

I let that sink in. That's what I wanted, no, needed to tell my son. I see Derek thinking about what I've said.

Then I return to the box. "You can have whatever you want in here. Find out about your mother. About me." So he closed the lid and returned to his seat across from my desk, but I stayed standing next to him. "Tell me what's on your mind?" I ask.

"I hated you for so long, now I'm not sure what to think. It's difficult to process."

"I'll go at your pace, but I'll always be here to talk to, to help you find yourself. That is if you want it." We have a pregnant pause before a knock on the door comes and Angel pops her head in. "Millie told me to come and say dinner's ready." Then she leaves as we get up and go to our delicious meal. Can't wait for the tiramisu.

****

After we say 'grace', dinner is served. We introduce Angel and she stays quiet, not knowing her place here. Heck, neither do I. Something got my attention as I quickly glance up at the window and notice a couple of flashing lights then they fade. Must be an ambulance or something. As we eat we all relaxing a bit. I do notice Derek take three helpings of spaghetti. I take two. When we get to the tiramisu, well... it is... Well, no words can describe how good it was. I mean it is really good. The whole meal is delicious! Derek then says to us all, "tell your friend that this meal is the best I've ever had, including fried gator."

Angel gives a snarly face, scrunches her nose, and replies, "Fried gator? Yuck." Then shakes her head and we all laugh. Yea, it sounds bad. Just then, the door is kicked open and a man is standing at the door. *Big Daddy!*

"Hands up. Nobody moves or I start shooting! Give me the girl and nobody gets hurt." Remind me to get a deadbolt.

Everybody's shaking. We get up slowly and I raise my hands in the air, as Millicent has sent Derek and Angel in the kitchen away from the line of fire. He has a gun pointed at my chest. I'm gonna need to think fast here. *Lord help us. What do we do? I am not handing that girl over. NEVER!*

"There's no need for violence," I say to the man as I hold up three fingers behind my head, hoping Millicent sees my hand. She moves closer as I touch her backside. She digests my message. Then the man moves a couple of steps closer. "I said NO MOVING." He's about fifteen feet away. I move in front of him to block his line of sight between him and Millicent and the kitchen. I've moved my hands again behind my head like I'm being arrested. Then I put my first finger up behind my head so Millicent can only see.

"Again, there's no need for violence. We're a peaceful family. You don't want to hurt anyone," I say, hoping to have him calm down. He replies curtly, "I..want..the..girl. She's already been paid for. Now give her to me NOW!" He yells with the gun still pointed at me. I put two fingers up. Then I think of Millicent, Angel, and Derek. *My family.*

"Did you kill her mother?" I ask hoping for a confession. If we get out of this, may be the police can use it?

"Yep," he declares pridefully. "I used her but she became worthless to me. But Angel will bring big bucks on the streets. So young. So innocent. Not too young, yet young enough. Perfect for my plans." He's a worthless piece of junk. I move a little closer. Then I put my third finger up and dive on the floor. A shot rang out and as I look up from the floor, I see blood.

Chapter 21
Millie

When that creep crashed through our door I immediately sent Angel and Derek in the kitchen out of harm's way. We're going to protect Angel and Derek at all costs, because of this guy… this nutcase is after her. Marcus is standing by my side, then taps by back waist near my weapon, then moves in front blocking Big Daddy's line of sight with me. Then Marcus held up three fingers. I then know what he wants. One… Two… I slowly grab my weapon so that maniac doesn't see me. I've never shot anyone before, but when I go to target practice and even renew my Concealed Carry Permit, I am a dead eye. I never miss. But this is got to be a quick shot. I'm not scared. More angry than anything but I have to maintain control of my emotions. I get only one shot and if I'm not fast enough, or I miss, then we're dead and Angel will be forever gone. And I can't let that happen. Fortunately, my husband is brilliant. And on three he hits the floor and as if in slow motion Big Daddy starts to move his weapon towards me. I quickly draw my gun out and fire. BANG! Then I hear a scream. I stare in front of me to see this creep down and Marcus on the floor looking up. He yells, "Everyone okay?"

I glance back at Angel and she's being covered by Derek who's protecting her. *Protecting her.* Then it hits me. He's a part of the family too. I immediately holster my weapon and Marcus gets up, kicks Big Daddy's gun away, and stares down at the invader. I step forward. Then an amazing thing happens. Marcus takes off his shirt, leans down at him and I step up right behind my husband to see the man I shot. For me, I don't feel a thing.

    "Derek. You there? Call 911!" my husband cries out. Marcus gets on his knees, takes his shirt and applies pressure on the upper shoulder area. As I peer down I notice that I didn't hit what I aimed for. We're taught to shoot to kill, but for some reason, I hit his shoulder area. He's down, somewhat conscious. The funny thing is I never miss. I aimed for the heart but got the shoulder. Whew. *Thank God.*

    "I'm applying pressure to stop the bleeding, so stay still," Marcus tells the man. Then Marcus leans closer as I step closer to hear. I want to know what he says. "Today you may or may not die. I don't know, " Marcus continues. "But do you know where you'll be when you do die?"

    "Cough. Cough. Cough." The man is coughing and is trying to get up but Marcus holds him down. He's too weak now because the his blood is all over the floor. Then I hear sirens from a distance. "Everyone needs Jesus. Even you. Do you want to know him now? Because your time may have run out." Marcus is witnessing to the guy that almost killed us! Big Daddy coughs some more, then goes unconscious, but I can see his chest go up and down. He's breathing. Just then, two police officers with guns drawn come in. I watch and observe my husband then glance behind to see Derek and Angel witnessing the whole thing.

****

    About two hours later, we've been interviewed separately and together and Sandra Coblentz arrived an hour ago. Our unexpected guest was taken away in an ambulance almost immediately after the police got here.

Sandra, after having confiscated my gun, whispers to me, "Millie? I can't officially tell you anything but this will be a clean shoot." She gets up and walks away. Both Marcus and I are sitting on our couch. I eye Angel sitting at the island in the kitchen. She looks numb. I get up and go to her as Derek goes to his dad.

"Okay?" I ask Angel.

Angel nods her head and we hug each other hard. I'll do anything for my child. Then, Jill and Josie come in, talk with Sandra, then comes to me.

"Millie, you sure know how to do it right." Yea.

"Jill? What's gonna happen?"

"Well, first of all, we're going to get you permanent custody of Angel, if that's okay with you Angel." Angel gives a slight smile, glances back at Jill and replies to her, "that would be great."

"I've checked with the..." Just then Greg walks in with his badge on and blue jeans.

"Sorry, Sandra. I'm not taking your case, but Deek asked I come and let you know that there will be federal charges as he probably is connected indirectly with that gang we busted up back in Virginia. Want to coordinate?" Greg's family was threatened by them last fall. And, Deek is FBI in the area and has recently been coming to church since moving up here.

Sandra replies, "Of course." And they go off to talk.

A while later, the police are still here gathering evidence. It's cold outside, but as I look out the window I see the police tape around and behind the tape are a bunch of our friends. Mavis, Nathan, Sofia, Charlotte, Kyle. I don't see Jared, But I do see Amy. I also see Nick, and I see Josie who must have gone back outside to be out of the way. We need to see her.

Still a bit later, the police have trickled out and it's almost midnight and everyone's gone home. We say our goodbyes to Derek who has a story to tell back at the dorm. Apparently, Marcus had called the coach and asked him to give Derek a break on curfew. I guess a former All-American linebacker in the Hall of Fame and is chaplain of the team can have some pull. But as I gaze around my house and... well? It's a mess. We've also been told we need to find another place to stay tonight. And, I believe getting a home invader is a reason for Angel to miss school tomorrow. Just then Amy comes in. I didn't notice she's still here.

"Millie? Marcus? Why don't you come and stay out with us. Grab a few things. We have the room. I'm sorry Jared wasn't here. He's at the house getting everything ready for you. Stay at the ranch as long as you need to." Such friends. Friends and family. I look at Angel, then Marcus and we all nod in agreement. Let's go.

****

"Millie, this is Jill," I hear as I've answered my phone the day after what the newspaper calls this morning "Gun-Toting Pastor's Wife Shoots Invader". I hate the publicity. *I just hate it!* I can relate to Sofia and Nathan who crave privacy.

"Hi Jill, how's it going?" I ask, hoping she has some news for us about whether I'll be charged or some news on Angel.

"I'm good actually. Been busy. I wanted to update you on everything."

"Okay, do I need to get Marcus?"

"No, I've got just a short period of time as I'm in court in about forty-five minutes."

"Okay. Shoot." Oops. Shouldn't have said that.

"Very funny."

"First, Big Daddy AKA George Kelly has been charged. He's going to recover. For some reason, he's confessed to everything on Angel's mother and even some things the cops don't even know about. And he wants to see if Marcus will visit with him. Know anything about that? I don't recommend it as your attorney." She's been very protective of me ever since college.

"Let's just say Marcus witnessed to him last night before he lost consciousness."

"You're kidding right?"

"Nope."

"I'll be a monkey's aunt. Okay. Well it's his call then, but I suggest that two go. May need another staff member but not you."

"I'll tell him, Jill. What else you got." I'm getting anxious here.

"Oh yeah. The prosecutor and I came up with a solution and George has agreed to terminate his parental rights and give sole custody to you and Marcus. So there are no barriers to you gaining permanent custody and eventual adoption. My guess you get to adopt her with my connections in about a month or so. That's unusually fast but I have connections like I told you before." Wow, that's great news!

"Cowabunga!" I yell out as everyone is now gathering in Amy's kitchen near me. I give a 'thumbs up' to everyone that now includes Marcus, Angel, Nick, Jared, and

Amy.

"Millie, I have to go, but tell everyone 'hi' from us."
I'll see you later Hun." Then she's gone.

I relay the information to everyone and Angel jumps
up and down, happy that she gets her home. Jared also
mentions he arranged for a cleaning service to come in and
do our house from top to bottom once the police release the
crime scene. Good times.

Chapter 22
Transcript from Interview by
Famous TV Christian News Journalist
Mona Rogers

Mona: Good morning and thank you. Today on *Christian Beat* we're in football city Canton, Ohio where we're sitting down for the only interview of Millie and the Reverend Marcus Jenkins, who have become nationally known for stopping an intruder from entering their house by using a gun. This incident created a national uproar on the debate of gun control and also among the Christian community on using weapons to defend themselves. To recap, a known prostitution and drug kingpin, George Kelly was there to kidnap their foster daughter, whose name we withhold because she is a juvenile. We can say this because he confessed to the crime of home invasion, attempted kidnapping, and the murder of the child's mother. For the record, the Jenkins' have stated that they will not be doing any other interviews and will not comment on the shooting. And thus far they have refused any interviews publicly, until today. Thanks for being here.

Marcus: Thank you for talking to us.

Mona: Now you declined to speak to the media frenzy through all of this and only decided to agree to an interview with us because you and Millie wanted to set the record straight, correct?

Millie: Yes, most of the news media have been wrong and inaccurate about the actual facts of the case.

Mona: Fake news then?

Marcus: You could say that, but I pretty much think that the term 'fake news' is a politically charged statement and we prefer not to publicly state our political views.

Mona: So what are some of the inaccuracies? Can you list a few you've heard?

Marcus: There's been speculation about the state of our marriage, which is nobody's business, and our church as being weird or a cult, which is ridiculous. One reporter alleged that I make a million dollars a year. I wish. I hate to disappoint anyone but that's not even remotely close. We make ends meet, but our income is a private matter. There have been reports of Millie.. uh... Millicent carrying three guns, two knives, and practices ninja-like techniques. Someone even posted on social media that my wife paints her face blue and runs around with a sword. Just crazy stuff. One headline speculated I force my wife to do these things. That is ludicrous. I can't force her to do anything. And anybody that's married should know better.

Mona: (laughs) So the police have cleared you Millie of any wrongdoing correct?

Millie: Yes, they found it as a 'clean shoot' as we've been officially informed through our attorney. By the way, for the record, I don't paint my face. I barely wear makeup.

Mona: (Laughs) Yea, I can see that. Now briefly tell us Marcus, what happened?

Marcus: Well it's really not much to tell other than the suspect kicked down our door in as we were finishing dinner. He indicated that he wanted to take our foster daughter to sell for prostitution, and we just were not going to let that happen. So I moved to block him from my family and used hand signals behind my back to indicate to Millicent or. Uh... Millie. When I ducked, she fired her weapon. He was hit in the shoulder.

Mona: I'm not clear. How did Millie here know what you were doing?

Marcus: Well. I trust her completely. I just knew. Call it instinct. We call it divine intervention. I just knew what my wife would do when I got out the way.

Mona: He had a gun pointed at your chest right?

Marcus: Right.

Mona: Were you scared?

Marcus: Interesting question. A person close to us asked me the same question. At the time I wasn't. I knew what I had to do... what we had to do to protect our loved ones. Again, call it instinct. We call it divine intervention.

Mona: Now rumor has it you witnessed to him as he was laying there bleeding on your floor.

Marcus: That's correct. I took off my shirt and applied pressure to his shoulder to help stop the bleeding then I called out for... someone with us... to call 911. Then I did. I felt compelled to do that.

Mona: Amazing! You actually witnessed to your attacker.

Marcus: Yes. Aren't Christians called to do just that?

Mona: Yes. I see that. And how did that make you feel Millie?

Millie: At first I was in a little shock. Shooting someone is not something you take lightly, but I had been well-trained and I maintained control. But as to Marcus witnessing to him, I was very proud of my husband. Very proud.

Mona: Forgive me. Millie. I can't imagine how you could pull a trigger of a gun knowing that you could have killed him.

Millie: To be honest, Mona, I've processed the incident a hundred times in my head. I regularly shoot at the range to keep my instincts sharp. If someone owns a weapon, then he or she should be prepared to use it. I've always been taught to shoot to kill. That day I shot to kill. I still can't understand why I hit the shoulder and not the chest. I was 12 feet away and should not have missed. Now I'm not saying I wished for a different outcome. I absolutely do not. But I cannot explain why I missed.

Marcus: Divine intervention Millicent.

Mona: Back to the perpetrator. How did he find you? From the police reports they had a car at the house and then originally they thought he left the state.

Marcus: Well. We had been taking our... foster daughter to church and someone posted a picture of her online, without permission. We didn't know it as I'm not a social media fan, and well that's how he found out where she was. As for the police, he created a diversion near our house to get the officer to leave. Then he made a move on our house. I don't blame the police. They did the best they could and this guy was slippery.

Mona: So someone in the church gave it away.

Millie: Apparently so.

Mona: On a more personal topic I noticed earlier you call your wife 'Millicent' Marcus. Why?

Marcus: I guess her given name is a term of endearment for me. Some call their wives 'honey', 'sweetheart', or 'sugar bear'. My Millicent is a force of nature. I'm proud to use her name.

Mona: (laughs) You seem to have a strong, loving marriage.

Marcus: We do. It's not without challenges but a

great marriage requires work. We do have a loving marriage that is Christ-centered.

Mona: How long have you been married?

Millie: Fifteen years. Sixteen in May. We got married the day after we graduated from graduate school here in Canton. Go Cavaliers!

Mona: (laughs) Okay! And, you met in college right?

Marcus: Yea. We met in undergraduate at U of Canton but we had different social circles. (laughs) She hated me at first. And I understand why. I was not the nicest of persons in college. After I got injured my senior year I was forced to take a hard, long look at what my life was to be. In grad school, it was a literal act of God to get her to even notice me.

Mona: Millie?

Millie: Well. It's not something I like to talk about much, but...

Mona: Now Millie…. Come on. America wants to know.

Millie: Okay. I admit it! I didn't care for Marcus in college, but when he got injured he changed and got saved, and I did too in a separate life experience. You could say that God changed both of us and He knew to put us together eventually.

Mona: Speaking of which Marcus you were an All-American linebacker here at the University of Canton right?

Marcus: Uh... yea I was until I got injured my senior year.

Mona: And you set some conference records and are in the Cavalier Hall of Fame right?

Marcus: Yes.

Mona: And Marcus, what was your undergraduate major?

Marcus: Physical education

Mona: Millie?

Millie: Psychology.

Mona: And Marcus you received a masters in theology here and Millie you received your masters in counseling right?

Marcus and Millie: That's right.

Mona: On a more serious note, one of the things I learned about you Millie is that you're unable to have children of your own is that correct?

Millie: Um.. yea that's right.

Mona: Many women suffer from this problem. I read that roughly ten percent of women in their childbearing years suffer from infertility. What is your specific condition if you don't mind me asking?

Millie: (tears) I usually don't talk about this very much.

Mona: I'm sorry if this is too difficult.

Millie: No it's okay. I guess if it helps others then okay. I was diagnosed with endometriosis as a teenager. The theory is that it's a birth defect. Unfortunately, I had a hysterectomy to correct it, but now there are other less invasive treatments. I don't think it was the best course of treatment in hindsight. I'm still not sure why, but health care wasn't the best in my area, and well… I guess you could say I didn't exactly grow up in an environment that was knowledgeable about such things. But God has a plan and I don't think we would be on the path we're on now if things were different. It's hard to know. Sometimes I find my mind wandering with regret for not having my own children but

since we have fostered now, my attitude has changed.
And, Marcus knew early on before we were married and still
loves me for who I am. That's also been very helpful.

    Mona: That's great and Marcus I know you're
proud of Millie for speaking out. Many women will take
courage from your words. And maybe a few men too.
Moving on. Millie? You also teach self-defense classes for
women. Doesn't Jesus say Christians should turn the other
cheek? How do you reconcile self-defense with that?

    Millie: I don't think Jesus calls us to be run over
every time we get hit on. Jesus respects women,
particularly strong ones. Society has in the past and even a
few people now treat women poorly and view us as weak.
And, maybe this is controversial but women should not be
afraid to prepare themselves in body, as well as mind and
spirit for life. We should not respond in anger and malice
though. That is the meaning of that verse about turning the
other cheek. Don't respond in anger. Now, in a world that
cares little to protect each other, believers need to be aware
of how to be able to defend themselves. Marcus tried to
convince our intruder to peaceably go away. He refused,
and we had to stop him to protect people, particularly a
child.

    Marcus: One thing to add. There is nothing Biblical
about treating our sisters in Christ as anything other than
equals in the eyes of God. We are to serve one another in
love. I think people take scripture and read it but don't
really study its meaning. I truly admire Millicent and the
women in our church and others who are strong and they
actually help the men to be better men and better
Christians. I know Millicent makes me better, both as a
pastor and as a man.

Mona: Well, I'm looking forward to following up on your ministry here in Canton. This is Mona Rogers and that's all the time we have today. Thank you for joining us and we'll see you on the *Christian Beat*.

Chapter 23
Marcus
Early February
Super Bowl Sunday

This Sunday is a glorious day, yet it's about zero degrees outside with blowing snow. Warm day for Ohio. That will keep the older members away though. Seriously, it gets cold in February but this is northeast Ohio. Again a Bahamas vacation would be nice now. The last couple of weeks or so have been active. We stayed at Jared and Amy's for a few days after the shooting while the cleaners came in and when we returned home I couldn't believe how clean it was. People from the church also brought food in and a lot of it. Thank goodness we have food. Millicent. I love her to death, but her cooking needs work. I have thought of giving us a present to take a cooking class together at the local community college or have Sofia do it. It seems our church friends came through again.

Josie also came and oddly, she, Morgan Davis, and Jasmine Jackson have become friends. Yesterday Millicent had the annual single women's retreat and they sat together, quickly becoming friends apparently. We'll see. Josie. She worries me. But I've put her in the Lord's hands. We also solidified a deal with our new assistant pastor and he will be introduced today to both services. We may have to go to three services and more staff if the church continues to grow. This week, our new assistant pastor will go with me to the jail to see George, formerly Big Daddy, who's now a believer. We'll also pay a visit to Jasmine's father, Joe. I have a job for him too. God moves in mysterious ways indeed. By the way, I've given Millicent a special project. Morgan Davis. Morgan has moved out of her parents into the cabin and is wandering through life. She will graduate in business and already has her real estate license, but she needs some motherly help. And, Millicent just may have the project for her.

As for Angel. She was the one in need, but I wonder if she was provided for Millicent and me to fulfill a need of ours. Regardless she is doing very well and the adoption will be finalized February 28th. All of the custody arrangements have been accelerated with the combined efforts of Jill, Josie, and even George. The national attention helped too. On a related note, we had a memorial service for Angel's mother so she could begin to have some closure for her. The church again came out in force the other day providing flowers and food.

Yesterday, while cleaning the house and getting some laundry done while Millicent and Angel went to the Singles Women's Conference at church, I received a flat package in the mail. I opened it to find an autographed picture of the rock group *Melting Squash*. David Salley, former college roommate of Nathan Moore and the lead singer known as 'Meat", also had a note in the envelope with the picture.

Dear Pastor Marcus,

   Nathan emailed me about your situation and the good news of getting a daughter and son. Congratulations. You helped me so much in college and I'm glad the church voted the way it did. Take courage, my friend. I hope to see you soon. We end our world tour in March then hit the studio in April. Nathan has us scheduled at ZON. Then we go on a summer tour in June, unless I change my mind. When I get in, I'll call so we can have some lunch like old times. Tell Millie I'm fine. Her last email said she worries about me. Tell her 'don't'. By the way, here's another souvenir for your office.

Rock on and God bless!
David

I removed the picture from the envelope, found a frame in the basement that had some stupid award in it. I took out the award and put the picture in the frame. And I plan to hang the picture up in my office.

Derek has been coming to church sitting near or beside Jasmine. And today is a special day. I get to baptize both of my children, Angel and Derek. Yep. Derek is now a believer. When I attended to George on my floor after the attack, Derek could not believe that I witnessed to him. He also couldn't believe I'd risk my life for him who almost ruined our family and he couldn't understand why I live the way I do. He has seen Millicent as how a woman should conduct herself, and I think he wants what he lacked in his life before. A mother who cares deeply about him. After my conversations with Derek, I can only conclude that Breanna almost resented Derek in some way, and tolerated his existence. But I'll never know, at least on this Earth. But he's quickly becoming a part of our family too. Last week he came to my office and we went to lunch and I witnessed to him. He accepted Christ right then and said to me, "You don't just say you have faith. You live it. I want that too. To live for something more than what I've been doing. I guess I want to know if God has a purpose for me?" I told him, "Of course he has a purpose. You are here for a reason. You came to find me for a reason. Your motives may have been less honorable, but God even used that for His purpose. So in order to receive Jesus, believe in Him. And receive Him in your heart. Then you have to die to self." And he did.

The attack became national headlines, which I hated. The media got it all wrong. They called Millicent 'mama ninja', 'Annie Oakley', and other names. She

actually hated using her weapon in self-defense but Millie
had no choice. It was either her or him. But in the end,
God intervened and they both made it. The media though
could care less. They even made fun of her Mama Bear
Self-Defense class and made snide comments about our
faith. My anger burned hot for a while. Gun rights debates
emerged. After seeing the media and TV coverage of the
shooting I became concerned about the reputation of the
church. After seeing me so down about it, Millicent called
her friend Mona Rogers, host of Christian Beat, to interview
us. Trusting my wife, I reluctantly agreed to it. I think it
went well and others, or the ones that count liked it, but time
will tell. But we decided to do that one interview and that
was it. No book deals, no nothing. We also tried to keep
Derek out of it to preserve our budding relationship and he
was grateful. And Mona, who is internationally renowned,
and is a former college classmate of Millie's and a student
of Jared's, agreed to come in and do it. After that, the
media moved on to some Hollywood breakup, or some
other more 'newsworthy' event.

Today is the Lord's Day again and while the
weather is bad, the mood is bright and warm. So needless
to say it's a big day. For a pastor, a baptism Sunday is
special, but today I get baptize my children, which makes it
extra special. And it's Super Bowl Sunday so I get to watch
the game! After the baptisms, the singing, and me
changing into my dry clothes and my t-shirt that says, "Don't
mess with my wife" I come out from the back and get up to
speak.

"My friends. Today has been a special day for our
church and for my family. Yes. My family is whole, thanks
to God. In addition to baptizing Angel and Derek, we were

blessed to also baptize eight others and had re-dedication ceremonies for others. God is good. All. The. Time. Amen and Amen." Applause and 'Amens' come from the congregation and I go on.

"Today I want for you, brothers and sisters to get up one by one, as you are lead, introduce yourselves, and tell us what blessings the Lord has given you the last couple of months. Then, we'll praise him for those blessings. I've already said that Millicent and my blessing has been Angel and Derek. Who else wants to go?"

Charlotte and Kyle stand as the mic is passed to them. Charlotte begins. "Most of you know that the last few months have been hard on us as I had some health problems dealing with Ellis' birth. We are thankful that he and I were miraculously healed by the Lord. And, we also want to announce that we plan to adopt as we are on the adoption list for several Christian agencies, including overseas ones. Praise God!" Applause rings out.

"Who else?" I ask.

Jared and Amy get up. Jared speaks to the audience saying, "I just want to praise God for healing our family in the midst of... challenges we've had. Amy has been a blessing as well as Robin, Greg, Jesse, and Sofia this past year. And of course our miracle baby Ellis. And we're blessed that Amy will be getting her certification as an exercise trainer in Ohio next month hoping to get on at the gym next door. And I don't if you've heard yet but at a called faculty meeting Friday, I was named Provost at the University so I am beginning a search for my replacement in a couple of weeks." More applause and 'Amens' come from the church body.

"Praise God and thank you, Derek. Anybody else?"

The person that surprises me is Morgan. She gets up timidly and I see her hands shaking. Morgan was one of the people that rededicated her life this morning. Today, Morgan is sitting next to Iris, Jasmine, Derek, and Josie is on the end. Three of the young women were sitting together at the Single Women's Retreat yesterday, or so Millicent told me last night. She met with them also to talk about the next projects.

"First, I want to apologize for my immaturity these last couple of years." She stops and tears are in Morgan's eyes. "I rededicated my life to the Lord today and commit to being in service to him. My grandfather died recently and while that was hard and we'll miss him, in that tragedy, I really took a hard look at my life and I wanted and needed a change. God has truly spoken to my heart lately and Millie is going to help me, and my new friends Jasmine and Josie." Morgan sits down tears rolling down her cheeks smearing her makeup. I hope her change sticks. I really do.

Miss Jenny Akers gets up. She's Nick's aunt. "Pastor. I want to thank the Lord that my nephew has returned safely home from his service to our country. His shoulder is recovering well with therapy though with all the screws in it he'll set off all the metal detectors at the airport." People laugh at her dry humor. Nick gets that humor from her.

"And I want to thank the Lord that I was able to recover from my recent bout with the flu which resulted in a brief stay in the hospital. Thanks again Marcus for the visit. And thank you, everybody, for the cards and to my new friend Mavis, thank you for your new friendship and support. Praise God." Jenny Akers sits down. Jenny is about sixty and used to be a school secretary before retiring a few years ago. Jenny is a beautiful woman and I'm amazed she's remained single. Jenny is a pearl. She's recently connected with Mavis, Charlotte's mom. Never married but considered the children at Canton Academy her kids.

I end the praise time by telling the congregation, "One other praise we have to thank the Lord for today is this. Before I begin the sermon, I want to introduce our new assistant pastor. On my right on the stage is a new face to many but not all. He's been around recently, but after talking with him and after much prayer, I believe that God has sent him to us for this purpose, and maybe other purposes. Major Nicholas Taylor, retired Army chaplain, has agreed to be my right hand and serve Freedom Church, working with youth, education, and whatever else we decide for him to do." Just then I heard a small cry. I peer up in the congregation where I see Josie get up and run out of the auditorium. I wonder why?

Epilogue
Marcus
About six years later or so

"She's too young, Marcus." Millicent tells me the day of our daughter's wedding. "Millicent, we've been over this. She's going to be fine and Jesse is a great young man. A Godly man. And, Angel will be a great teacher. She's certainly show her talents at the preschool center. She's been working there since she was fifteen. I'm so proud of her. And Jesse will be a great worship leader. He's already interning at the church." Both Angel and Jesse are getting married today and I'm performing the ceremony as well as giving the bride away. After we adopted Angel she became Frances Angel Jenkins and today she becomes Frances Angel Jenkins Walker. Jesse was adopted by Greg and took the 'Walker' name a few years ago. What a long name for a driver's license Angel will have. But she wanted to keep her original name because her mother named her that. I can respect her for remembering her birth mother that way. But, Millicent and Angel have become a mother-daughter team since she was adopted into our family. Yea they've had disagreements but it's been good. I have been a vigilant dad, by working to keep Jesse and Angel as far apart as possible, but it seems my plan didn't work out like I intended. Oh well. But I love my little girl who's now a woman of true character and virtue. And we gain a son-in-law. When Jesse came to me six months ago to ask for permission, I shook his hand and said 'yes', but then I squeezed his hand in my big grip, leaned over to him and discreetly told Jesse, "But if you intentionally hurt her, I'll hurt you." I'm still the protective dad. But, yea, they're both still in college, but young marriages are fine with me. People today sometimes wait too late, and well, I'm not sure that's the best. But that's not my business.

"Millicent," I respond as I glare at my beautiful bride who's in my office straightening my tie. "Everything's going to be fine. Jesse's a fine Christian man, and they'll have all of our support.   Besides, he's waited six years for this moment and she has too. After what they've both been through they deserve this." I put my eyebrow up, stare intently and with resolve at Millicent, and tell her in my husky voice, "And, he knows how I feel about how he will treat my baby." Millicent chuckles and continues to work on my tie. Today is a special day and I'm wearing my new suit and tie, but underneath my dress white shirt is my new t-shirt that says, "Daddy of the Bride." Angel gave it to me at the bridal shower last month. And, yea… she calls me 'Daddy', and I love it. She's called me that since we adopted her. Millie goes by 'Mama' and it suits her to a tee.

Jesse had his own family demons to conquer in that his biological father is currently in federal prison in Colorado, unrepentant to this day. He's refused to see Jesse and that was that. Angel, however, has struggled to forgive her father, even though he's a changed man. I've encouraged her to visit him and she did a couple of years ago finally. Things are better, but not perfect. I continue to visit him and Joe goes with me. Joe is Jasmine's dad. I quickly change the subject.

"Are Derek and his wife here with our new grand baby?" I ask hoping that the grandma Millicent will come out. Derek has two kids now, and he's a great father. It seems that being a new grandma has suited Millicent well.

Millicent hates the term 'grandma' but she still hasn't settled on a name yet. Some days it's 'Nana', other days it's 'Meemaw'. I don't care really. But I still can't believe I'm a grandfather at forty-six, but it is what it is. Derek. Derek has done a 180 since our first encounter and I believe God has great things in store for him. He's a financial wizard and has even taught financial awareness classes at church to help those whose debt has become an anchor in their lives. And he's helped a lot of people, including Millicent and me, prepare better for retirement. Many have benefited from Derek's talents including Jasmine and her mom, as well as other church members. And the funds Mr. Davis and others set up with the church have grown well under his guidance. That's what pays for both Jesse and Angel's education. Derek has a great wife and family, but that's a story for another day. Today is about my Angel and Jesse.

****

A few hours later we're wrapping up. The wedding went off with a hitch. The bride and groom are now on their way to honeymoon in the Bahamas after flying out of the Canton Airport, and everyone has had a good time. It was a traditional church wedding, and both Jesse and Angel decided to keep things simple. It was probably one of the most beautiful weddings I've ever attended or officiated. Simple yet elegant. Angel looked like...well... an angel. She's grown into a beautiful young woman and it showed today. David sang a couple of songs today. All of the family on the Moore side pitched in as well and it was certainly a family affair. Nathan provided the videographer and a sound person from his studio, and Sofia made the food. And there's a lot left over so we put it in the church kitchen to take home later. Good for Millicent and me as we will get to take a lot home.

After the wedding and reception, we finally get home, tired and somewhat exhausted from the week but I have a little energy left. I take my Vitamin B and other pills Millie gives me. As we get ready for bed, Millicent has that look in her sexy dark eyes that tells me what's she's thinking. I'm thinking it too. I've been thinking about it for most of the day now, especially when I saw my bride very nearly outshine Angel. So we close the bedroom door, turn out the light, and the rest is… well... no one else's business.

Millie's Homemade Laundry Detergent

Millie makes her own laundry detergent, based on a formula given to her by some Amish friends.

Ingredients:

65-ounce box Borax
55-ounce box of washing soda
1 Fels Naptha Laundry Bar (Some other
          brands are fine. Some of her friends use
          more than one bar, but Millie prefers not)
5-gallon bucket with lid
1 or 2 tablespoon measuring cup

Instructions:

Using a kitchen grater, grind the bar of Fels Naptha soap. Millie prefers to use a fine grater (like in a kitchen) to grate the soap. The smaller the pieces the easier it is to distribute through the laundry detergent. Set aside for now. In the five gallon bucket, pour a little of the Borax, then a little of the washing soda, then put a little of the grated soap. Repeat until done. Place top on the bucket and shake. Muscle may be required and Millie has enough of it, but Marcus could help as well. Store in a dry area with the lid on. When washing a load of laundry, use 1-2 tablespoons per a load of laundry and keep the measuring cup in the bucket. Some of Millie's Amish friends mix in scented laundry crystals. Others may want to but Millie prefers not. She doesn't like conflicting scents on her, but that's a personal choice. It's a choice though, but Marcus doesn't complain either but he never complains. Also, Millie does not guarantee the results of her formula and does not warranty or endorse specific brands or products.

Want More?

Read the Internationally selling prequels:

     Book 1 - The Second Choice
     Book 2 - A Matter of Trust
     Book 3 - The Foodies
     Book 4 - The Robin's Egg

See the bonus preview of the next book, "Josie's Journey"

Josie's Journey
(The Freedom Church Series)
Book 2

By Alex X. Bradbury

Chapter 1
Seven years Ago
Emails

TO: Josie
FROM: Myron
Subject: Hello from somewhere overseas

My Josie,

We got so little time to video chat together yesterday that I thought I would write a short email before I have to go on patrol. The news that you're pregnant is quite a surprise but I wouldn't change it at all. Are you and the baby okay? What's the sex? Have you been to the doctor? Details. Details.

I love you and when I get home we'll be married. I can't afford an engagement ring like you deserve but maybe I can make it up to you someday. I know we have had little time to talk but I want you to be the mother of my children. At camp here, the men and women are great, and I told our company chaplain about our situation and he suggested I fill out a will and change my beneficiary forms. I will do that as soon as we get back on patrol. I am due to come back to you soon on leave but I'll know more from the sarge soon. We were told this is a short mission. Remember I love you.

Love,
Myron
Date Sent October 25

TO: Myron
FROM: Josie
Subject: Hello from home

My Dearest Myron,

I know we haven't exactly done things the right way, but you are right. I wouldn't want to have any other man's child than yours. I love you so much. I can't wait to be your wife. I miss you terribly. It's been hard going to school and keeping this secret. My friends don't even know. But I had to tell my parents since I'm on their health plan and had to go to an OB/GYN. They think I'm nuts and went crazy. My mother is more concerned about what others will think. But I don't care. I'm staying in school and when I have the baby, I take classes online. Good thing my grandparents provided for my education, but I'll have to find a job. Sweetie? Don't worry about an engagement ring. I want you home safe. That's what matters. I worry every day about that. Please come home safe. I have to go to my parents tonight because they demanded I come. More lectures. More disapproving looks. I wish I could just… well… I just wish it was you and me and our baby.

To answer your questions, yes I've been to the doctor. It's too soon to tell about the gender or anything else. The doctor is a little concerned about my blood pressure, but I'll be fine. DO NOT WORRY about me. He gave me prenatal vitamins to take and I'm following his orders to rest when I can. Please don't worry about me. Again, I'm fine. You take care of yourself and come back to me. Soon, I'll send you a care package for Thanksgiving. I also attached to this email a picture of me my roommate took today. As you see I don't show yet. I figure I'm about twelve weeks along. I hope the picture motivates you to come home soon. Oh, how I love you so much. Take care.

        Love,
        Josie
        Sent October 26

TO: Josie
FROM: Myron
Subject: Coming home

Honey bunch Josie,

        Yep. We got word from our Sarge that we're probably going home on a brief leave during Christmas, but we don't have details. Oh, how I missed you. I couldn't print your picture out but I stared at it for a long time, and you're right it does motivate me. It seems to be cold there in Ohio. But you are beautiful as always. I've imprinted it on my mind and you are the light of my life. My everything. I live for you every day. I'm so lucky that you're in my life. Thank God, you're doing okay with the baby but I'm worried about that blood pressure issue. Please take care of yourself. You mentioned earlier about your parents. Please don't be too hard on them as you'll need them to help you through the pregnancy. But if they don't seek out my aunt's friend Millie Jenkins. She is at Freedom Church and will not judge you or me. Tell her that my Aunt Freda sent you. I think they used to know each other in college, but I don't

know. Freda's been sick from what I heard in her last letter.
         Gotta go. Patrol again. Life is tough here and hot.
I'd rather be near you and home. I love you always. Happy
Halloween. Don't eat too much candy. Bad for the baby.
Will call tomorrow.

         Love,
         Myron
         Sent October 31

TO: Myron
FROM: Josie
Subject: Missed you

Hey Myron,

I know you're busy but we missed our call. I love you and
want to make sure you're okay.

Love,
Josie
Sent November 2

TO: Myron
FROM: Josie
Subject: Missed you

Myron,

Are you there? I'm sure you got wrapped up on a mission
but if you get a chance, call me. I'm very worried. Please
call. I love you.

Love,
Josie
Sent November 3

TO: Ms. Josie Bailey
FROM: Captain Nicholas Taylor, US Army Chaplain
Subject: Corporal Myron Cannaday

Dear Ms. Bailey:

        I am not sure you are aware, but I wanted to
personally write to you to let you know about your fiance'
Myron. It is with deep regret and sorrow that I inform you
that Myron was killed while on patrol in Afghanistan. I
cannot give you specifics because of national security, but I
want to tell you that he confided in me that if something
happened to him, I should email you. I notified his mother
yesterday evening as well as a Pentagon representative. At
this time I'm not sure of the arrangements. As the chaplain
for the unit, I usually notify the next of kin as well as a

United States Army representative in the States, but Myron asked me to do something that, while not unusual, is uncommon. In his papers, he indicated I should notify you. Myron told me that you loved him and he loved you. He did love you. We found a picture of you and I sent it with his personal effects to his family along with a small Bible I gave him. As I told his mother the details are sketchy at this time, but what I know is that he died while on patrol. Unofficially, I am told by his Sergeant that he died saving the life of another soldier. While it may not offer much comfort to you I cannot think of another better way to die than to give one's life for another. Myron had several friends in the unit he served and was a good soldier. I wished I knew him better but on the few times I interacted with him, I found Myron to be a fine, Christian young man who was an example on how to live life to the fullest. He was dedicated and while other soldiers here are as dedicated, Myron stood out among others. His Sergeant stated to me that he wished he had more "Myrons" in his unit.

Again, I cannot tell you how sorry I am for your loss. I did not know him for very long as he was only here for a short tour and had been here a few months. For you, I can't imagine how you feel. I don't have to tell you it will be difficult to raise a child alone, but I pray you'll have help. I usually don't do this, but I have family in your area. Please get in touch with Jared and Sarah Moore. Myron said that you're a student at the University of Canton. It just so happens that Jared, my brother-in-law, teaches there. Tell him 'Nicholas' sent you. My sister is an incredible woman and if you seek her out, she will help in any way she can.

I wish I could offer more to you. But I hope and desire that you take care of yourself. Myron was worried about you and I can safely say that he would want you to be safe and take care of his and your child. Again, my deepest sympathies for your tragic loss.

Sincerely,
Capt., Nicholas Taylor, U.S. Army
Sent November 5

www.ingramcontent.com/pod-product-compliance
Lightning Source LLC
Chambersburg PA
CBHW060425130626
46555CB00005B/2226